SOUTH-SIDE ESCAPE ARTIST

To Joe
Enjoy the book *Ray*

SOUTH-SIDE ESCAPE ARTIST

An Unusual Tale of Transformation and Liberation

ϟ

All roads lead us to our spiritual destiny.
This is the bumpy version.

Ray Holthausen

St. Louis, Missouri

To my mother, Jeanine Holthausen,
and my grandmother, Anna Liess,
the two quiet forces in my life
who were always there for me.
I love you always.

PREFACE

I never thought I'd write a book. I'm sure it will be a surprise to many. It's been a surprise to me as well. Miracles never cease. The first question that comes to mind is where did it all come from? For me, this is the greatest mystery.

I'm a sixty four year old retired firefighter who lived, worked, and grew up in South St. Louis in the late 50's, 60's, and early 70's. I lived in the area known as the state streets and was raised by my mother and grandmother in a two-family flat a block and a half west of Grand Avenue. I graduated from Rose Fanning Grade School in 1969 and Roosevelt High School in 1973—nothing mysterious about that. It was a conversation with my next door neighbor many years later that would spark an idea that would eventually lead to a book.

What started out as a casual conversation, ended up as a powerful and meaningful story about her brother-in-law who suffered a severe stroke.

She explained that he was an alcoholic and that he and his family were at a point of extreme crisis when it happened. As she told me the story, what took me by surprise was her point of view regarding the incident.

She described the stroke as a blessing in disguise, stating that he was literally transformed into a different person. She went on to describe how the stroke diffused an extremely volatile situation within his family and summarized her story by saying, "It was like

God killed the ugly part of his brain." It was that last statement that really caught my attention. I couldn't stop thinking about it.

Seeing something good evolve out of extreme loss became the seed idea for The South Side Escape Artist. The story of a character who ultimately experiences a transformation through devastating personal tragedy.

I started to write the narrative more than twenty years ago shortly after that unexpected conversation with my neighbor, but gave up on the idea soon after. I returned to it months later, but made little to no headway. After several unsuccessful attempts to produce anything meaningful, I threw the manuscript in a drawer and forgot about it. It was an unfinished dialogue that lacked clarity and direction. I dismissed it and moved on with my life.

Fast forward twenty years later. . .

While in a phone conversation with my cousin, she mentioned that she was interested in getting a reading from a psychic. I told her about a bookstore where the employees did psychic readings and asked if she was interested.

Three days later we met in the parking lot of the bookstore and made our way in.

Once inside, we came upon a young lady standing in front of a group of attentive listeners. Her name was Melina, and she announced to the crowd that she would do a spontaneous quick read for anyone who was interested.

Many hands raised, and Melina was quick to respond to all the volunteers. There were no places left to sit down, so my cousin and I stood in the back and listened while Melina responded to the many requests. My cousin and I eventually raised our hands, and after Melina did a reading for my cousin, she did a short reading for me.

The first thing she said to me was, "I see you as a Roman." The comment along with the reading didn't reveal anything significant that I could relate to. I made no direct connection to anything relevant going on in my life at the time, so I dismissed the comment along with the reading and moved on with my life.

It wasn't until about a week later that I realized that the main character in the book I started more than twenty years earlier was named Roman. This realization prompted me to re-discover and re-examine the text.

Two years later, this re-discovery led to a story which eventually grew into a thirty-one chapter book just recently completed in September of 2018.

My goal in writing this book was to write a once-upon-a-time-in-South-Saint-Louis story that reflected a very unique and memorable time and place. It represents my best attempt to recapture a fictional version of some of the memories, values, and characters of that time.

Having a career in emergency services has also given me many unique experiences to draw upon. Hopefully these combined elements have been blended into a story that you find original, entertaining, and fun.

Although the story is fiction, I tried to make it as real as possible drawing from experiences, friends, and characters I've known throughout my life. Great liberties were taken to make the story as rich and entertaining as possible. After all, that's what good fiction is all about.

The influence of South Saint Louis has profoundly affected many of us who lived and grew up there. I believe that where you come from always stays with you. I hope you find the story to be as interesting and unusual as the circumstances that prompted me to write it.

Many talented people have come to my assistance in the process of writing this book. I would like to take this time to thank them. The feedback I received from all of them has been invaluable.

I would like to thank my editor, Donna Brodsky. Your expertise, dedication, professionalism, and passion have helped me to bring this story to life. I can't thank you enough.

Also I would like to thank my book designer Carolyn Vaughan for her artistic expertise and great attention to detail. The cover designs she produced were absolutely amazing! I feel fortunate to have made contact with so many talented people.

Also a special thanks goes out to Melina Valdejo, Alice Wells, Al Estes, Calvin Marsala, Charlie Granda, Sandra Holthausen, Vicki Main, Pete Ahl, and Dr. Bridget Long—all of whom offered valuable insight in the early stages of this writing. Many thanks to all of you.

Respectfully submitted,
Ray Holthausen

SOUTH-SIDE ESCAPE ARTIST

An Unusual Tale of Transformation and Liberation

✕

All roads lead us to our spiritual destiny.
This is the bumpy version.

Ray Holthausen

CHAPTER 1

Please forgive me for starting this story from a point so deeply buried in the past, but time and poor health have so clouded my memory that a visitation seems the only viable means of restoration. It is not to my surprise, however, that I find myself in a state of hesitation. The past for me is not a pleasant place to be. Even now, I spend as little time there as possible. And as the old saying goes, "Better to let sleeping dogs lie," for this sleeping dog was a pit bull, and a volatile one at that!

I am reminded just now of the story of Frankenstein and the dilemma that's faced with the making of such a creature. The raising of the dead is, of course, the first issue at hand. I don't have to tell you that a great responsibility goes along with such an undertaking, for it is only in the realms of imagination that these kinds of things take place—at least before today. After all, the conquering of life over death could very well be what this twisted little excursion is all about. And yet, I think about the tragedy surrounding such a character, and I ask myself with my hand on the switch, "Should I do it? Should I zap him back to life?"

Or maybe I should just . . . let it be. You see, this is my dilemma of the moment, for time is running out for this tired old man whose decrepit physical condition has aged him to well beyond his years. But with the prospect of an enlivened return also comes a sense of some ground-expanding possibilities. There well might be a story to tell. At least this is my sense of the moment. So please bear with me, and please be patient, for this ground I am about to walk unnerves me even as I speak. So let us walk together, shall we, as we travel through this graveyard of yesteryear in search of a past life that may be better off left to the dead. But before we begin, it seems both necessary and appropriate for me to express a heartfelt thank you. Your company is not only appreciated but quite possibly indispensable, for to say that I'm uncertain of such a journey would be an understatement of the highest magnitude.

Even now, the thought of uncovering such dark possibilities brings a tremble to my hand and a shiver to my spine. I can assure you that a hand on my shoulder is a welcomed reassurance. So let us look now to what lies ahead, and let us walk cautiously as we do, for there are no guarantees here, I hope you know that—no guarantees and no assurances other than the comfort of a fellow traveler who like me chooses to walk this narrow path of uncertainty.

So all warnings aside, let me state it for the record here and now, that even though I find it necessary to awaken such a character, great reservations still linger. For with his awakening comes a whole Pandora's box of memories. So let us start carefully, with maybe just a nudge, so as not to piss him off.

I would like to say in his defense, however, that even though he was branded by some as a killer, it wasn't 100 percent his fault. And it most certainly was not the source of his nature.

You see, the main character, a tragic and tortured soul, was haunted and tormented by ghosts. Darkened spirits chose at their discretion to wander in and out of his mind at will. Invading little monsters of the mind, running free, unguarded, and unchecked like little innocent children armed with daggers, playfully slicing his mind into whatever channeled direction they so chose.

And where was he as he watched these internal little horror stories? After all, who is responsible for the nightmare?

An interesting word, is it not? *Nightmare*—a dark horse charging out of control through the dark and stormy clouds of a lost soul's mind. Yes, he was a nightmare to many—their worst nightmare ever, if ever the truth be known. So it is here that I resurrect him, for it is also fair to say that he lived there for much of his life. Haunted, as they say, by the dark spirit of anger, the dark spirit of resentment, the dark spirit of vengeance, and the dark spirit of retribution. The gates where they once entered and roamed free have since been closed. And with the closing of those gates brought the close to an out-of-control life.

I would also like to point out just how dangerous and degenerative a moment like this can be. And it all stemmed from one momentary loss of self-control. That's all it takes to start the process of destruction: a harsh word, the throw of a punch, the stabbing of a knife, the lighting of a match, the push of a button—and all of it motivated by the desperate attempt to free one's soul from the incarceration of the moment. The future of the world could very well hang by just such a moment. For it was just such a moment that defined the terms of his life, and it was just such a moment that led him to a miracle.

As you have probably already guessed, both he and I are one and the same. I speak of him now from a great distance, and to a large degree that's true. But there was once a time when the lines of separation were not always so clear—hence my reluctance to go back.

So let us take a deep breath, and let us throw caution to the wind as we brush the dirt from the headstone of yesteryear. And with pickax and shovels in hand, off we'll go like grave robbers to dig into the rubbled remains of a dead and discarded past, a past ripe with the stench of confusion and avoidance. For I must confess,

there's also a don't-look-a-gift-horse-in-the-mouth sense of gratitude for having survived.

So you see, there it is. Despite my reservations, the deep urge of
curiosity still pushes me for answers, even after all these years. So let
the contradictions continue! For it is here, with the resurgence of a
once-dead character, that the story really begins.

As I remember . . .

CHAPTER 2

My father died when I was twelve. That's when my mother said I decided to become a bum. This observation on her part wasn't revealed until many years later. I only tell you this now because my memory seems to function in bits and pieces, and I can only bring it to you the way I remember it.

I start here because she always felt like this was a pivotal turning point in my life. There were memorable times in my life when she would say, "If your father were alive, things would have gone much differently for you." To that I can only say, "Who knows?" But enough with excuses, it's time to move on.

My birth name is Roland—Roland Lee Highmark to be exact—but everybody in my neighborhood called me Roman. Apparently, the nickname was given to me by my father. I always assumed he gave me the name to instill within me a kind of ideal or high-minded symbol of perfection he expected me to live up to: the macho Roman warrior who conquered anything and everything in his path. I was proud of the name; I felt like it made me special. It fueled childhood fantasies of courage, loyalty, immortality, and indestructibility.

I didn't find out the real meaning of my nickname until I was eleven years old. I was eating dinner at the kitchen table with my mother, father, and brother one day, when curiosity about the origin of my nickname came to mind. In the spur of the moment, I asked rather innocently, "Dad, why did you start calling me Roman?"

He looked up from his dinner plate, swallowed his hunk of meatloaf, and said, "When you were a toddler, you used to roam and wander around like a lost puppy. I used to always say to your mother, 'Roland is roamin' around the house again.' "

"You roamed around the house so often, I started calling you Romin' Roland. After a while, I started calling you Roman for short instead. The name suited you better anyway, so that's how the nickname stuck."

I was devastated. Oh well, so much for immortality, courage, and indestructibility. Anyway, that's how I came to be called Roman.

I grew up in South St. Louis. We lived in the area of the state streets in a two-family flat just west of Grand Avenue. It was a working-class neighborhood with bars, bakeries, confectionaries, butcher shops, and an occasional drug store on almost every corner. I spent my time hanging out in the streets, parks, alleys, and schoolyards of that area. Life was pretty much contained to the neighborhood, but it was more than enough at the time. The kids I knew and ran with went to the same schools, shared the same values, and enjoyed the same social contacts.

It was a life as normal as anybody else's, but that was before my father introduced me to "the rules." From that point on, everything changed.

Looking back, I believe my dad knew something was wrong. I was the youngest in the family and his greatest concern. He wanted me to be prepared for life. He wasn't outwardly sick at the time, but I think he somehow knew his time was limited. He knew my education would soon be left up to me. "The rules" would end up being his last and final gift before he passed on.

Shortly after my father died, I moved to the basement. It was quiet and isolated, with a back door that allowed me to come and go as I pleased. That was just the way I liked it. I was always a loner by nature, and being away from everyone else in the house suited me.

My mother used to say my dad's death changed me. Looking back, I'd have to say it probably did. I watched for nine long months while the cancer slowly sucked the life out of him. I watched him weaken, decline, and suffer until death came along and put him out of his misery.

My dad was a fighter, a force of nature. He fought until he couldn't fight anymore. He always used to say to me, "Son, if you're going to go down, go down swingin'." That's just what he did. He took the pain and indignity of death, and he never complained—not once. It was hard to watch. I never felt so helpless.

I didn't cry when it all went down. My dad would never approve of such a thing. I just stood there next to him—looking at him. The last thing he said was my name. When the end came, I hugged him with tears in my eyes, and then just walked away. I never saw him again.

My mother tried to console me, but to no avail. The end was a reality I never before had to face. It was a reality I couldn't understand. It made me angry. I couldn't believe anything was capable of taking down my dad. He worked like a dog all his life, and what did it get him? Now he was gone.

My mother went to work immediately after his passing. There was no funeral, no service, no whoop-de-do, and no la-de-da. My dad would have none of it. He was a realist: no god, no religion, no after-life fairy tales. He used to say, "Son, no goose ever laid a golden egg, and if it did, it died with a stretched-out ass." His life was hard, and it hardened him as well.

My dad came from a line of hard drinkers and heavy gamblers. He grew up working in the shipyards down on the river, and he learned real fast to fight for whatever he had to. He was quick-minded, quick-tempered, hot-blooded, and cold-natured, and nobody, but nobody messed with him.

He used to say to me, "Son, respect is just like money. You got to work to earn it. And just like money in the bank, it'll grow into a reputation. And that'll work for you, too, if ya got balls enough to live by the rules."

"What rules?" I asked him one day. I had no idea what a loaded question it was.

His answer came quick, a lightning-flash crack across the face—not hard enough to hurt, but more than enough to get my attention.

"If you're gonna have your head up your ass, at least have sense enough to keep your hands out of your pockets. By the way, that's rule number one."

He had my undivided attention. I took my hands out of my pockets—and listened.

"Rule number two," he went on is, "look your opponent over. Size him up.

"Look at his hands, his size, his feet, his eyes, scars, tattoos, fingernails, anything that will tell you what this guy's about. Is he heavy, light, solid, or in shape?

"Is he big-boned or athletic? And what's he dressed like? Is he wearin' slippery soled shoes? Does he wear a watch or a ring—and if so, on what hand—'cause you can almost bet that's the hand he'll try to drill you with. But don't count on it.

"Then there's who is he with, and what do they look like? Are they carryin'—and if so, what?

"Which brings us to rule number three: If you don't know, let it go—'cause it ain't worth dyin' over, and tomorrow is another day. And with a new day comes a new opportunity, hopefully when they don't expect it—like when they're standin' at the urinal and both hands are occupied, or when they reach inside their pocket for their wallet or their car keys.

"And if it don't feel right, get your ass outta sight—'cause your instinct is usually right, and you're a damn fool if you wait around long enough for a reason. Remember! It's always *your* choice. You choose the time and place!

"That's rule number four, by the way, which ties in to rule number five: the element of surprise. Use it—every chance you get. Always, I mean always, try to take the first shot and make it count—'cause a good first shot can be the last if you do it right, and why not get it over and done with? A clean kill, that's what you're lookin' for. And if the first shot don't finish him, make sure the next ten do.

"Always remember, it's all about a *quick take out*. And if you can't do it with your hands or your feet or your fists or your teeth, use accessories. Pick up a chair or a brick or a rock or a stick—anything to win. And don't wait until you're in trouble to do it. Save your compassion for church, or you'll end up in heaven faster than you realize—and you know what kind of bullshit that is!

"Remember, you always want to make sure he thinks twice about whether he should come after you. And don't forget to remember his face—'cause the day might come when you once again cross paths. And if he's afraid of you, it might create a hesitation you can use to your advantage. So pay attention!

"There's always something to watch out for. For example, never, I mean *never*, tangle with a guy whose fist is the size of your head. Stay away from confrontations like that!

"Ya see, it's all about gettin' on top and stayin' there until it's over. Believe me, it's the only place to be, 'cause there's no such thing as a fair fight or a dirty one either. And winning is everything when you consider the alternative.

"Which brings us to the final rule: Abandon all the rules. You see, each situation is different, and there's no prize for second place. So once you learn all the rules, forget about 'em. They're all bullshit anyway. Just keep your eyes open and your head clear, and be aware. *Be aware!*"

So I learned the rules and lived by them as best I could for a number of years. However, there was one rule I learned on my own that the old man forgot to mention: Win or lose, it always hurts. This became my *golden rule*. You see, this rule gave me the insight to steer clear of almost any potential problem before it became one.

I was always smart enough to know that I wasn't a tough guy, at least not like the old man. But sometimes I got to the point where I just didn't care. . . .

Just so you know, "I don't care" can be a dangerous place to be. But like I said, I didn't care. You see, not everything my dad gave me was good. But right or wrong, good or bad, he did the best with what he had. . . . And I'll always love him for that.

CHAPTER 3

I got into my first fight when I was eleven. I was playing touch football in the alley with the older guys in the neighborhood. Normally, I wouldn't have been allowed to play, but they were short one player, and that was my way in. I was now on the same team with the toughest guy in the neighborhood. His name was Rubin. Rubin liked to fight. He was a head taller than me and about two years older. Rubin wasn't big for his age or physically superior in any way. His secret weapon was the hate he had inside. It turned him into a monster.

No one knew why Rubin was the way he was. He grew up with his grandmother, who either couldn't control him or didn't care enough to try. Beyond that, Rubin was a mystery that couldn't be trusted. You can't trust crazy, and you couldn't trust Rubin—but I didn't know that at the time. Rubin was also respected and feared in the neighborhood, and I looked up to him. I was being allowed to run with the "big dogs," at least for an afternoon, and I wanted to be accepted. I was the runt of the group, with everybody else being bigger, badder, older, and cooler. I wanted to be a part of that club.

Our opponents were from a neighborhood on the other side of the park. It was more than just a football game. Our pride was at stake, as was theirs. It made the competition intense. As the game progressed, it got dirtier and more aggressive. Late hits and trash talk eventually led to fistfights and a free-for-all.

I was in way over my head on the bottom end of a beatdown when I remembered my dad's teaching. I picked up a metal trash can lid from one of the nearby ash pits and swung it around in the direction of my opponent. The rim of the lid caught him right in the chops. It stopped him dead in his tracks. I continued swinging wildly at anybody who got close until the fight was over. I didn't win the fight, but I didn't lose it either.

From that moment on, I was accepted. I now had a free pass that nobody else in the neighborhood had: I was allowed to run with the older crowd. Rubin started calling me "Trash Man," and the name stuck. I was in.

It didn't take long to find out that "in" ain't all it's cracked up to be. A few days later, Rubin came to his newly formed crew with another challenge. He said he got us another fight with the same bunch we fought only days before. We were gonna meet up with them in the park at noon the next day.

Rubin recognized immediately that nobody in the group was too excited by the prospect of another confrontation. He quickly followed up by saying that anyone who didn't show would answer personally to him. This was a no brainer as far as I was concerned. I was more afraid of Rubin than anybody on the other side of the park. I was also the newest member of the group; I felt like I had no other choice than to follow through. Once again, I was in over my head.

The last time we went around, I got lucky. I knew that the guy I bashed with the trash can, whoever he was, would probably be seeking revenge. *What to do?* I had until noon the next day to figure it out. I remembered my dad's advice: the element of surprise—use it every chance you get.

The answer appeared like magic. I was looking through my closet when I found one of my Little League aluminum tee-ball mini-bats far in the back. I borrowed one of my older brother's jackets, put it on, and slid the bat up the oversized sleeve. I cupped my hand around the end of the bat and looked in the mirror on the closet door. The bat was completely hidden. It was small, light, easy to swing, and easy to conceal.

Still, I was scared; that night, I could hardly sleep. I laid in bed, staring at the ceiling. *How did I get myself into this?*

I woke up the next morning and couldn't eat. I stayed in my room all morning until it was time to leave. As I walked through the kitchen on my way out the back door, my mother looked at me strangely. She knew there was something about me that was not quite right.

"Why are you wearing your brother's jacket?" she asked.

I could feel the suspicion in her tone. I turned around and said, "He won't mind. Besides, Rocky's jacket is warmer than mine."

She didn't question my reasoning; and, more important, she didn't notice the bat up my sleeve. My confidence was growing.

The first person I met up with was Stretch. Stretch was crazy, too, but in a different way than Rubin—not as hateful. Rubin and Stretch were best friends. They had one thing in common: They were both shit-disturbers by nature. Neither one of them could help it. It was just the way they were.

Stretch's claim to fame was climbing up the sign pole of the local Jack in the Box with a broomstick he painstakingly fabricated into a giant arrow. After reaching the top, he jammed the arrow through Jack's oversized plastic head. This was one of Stretch's famous statements to the neighborhood.

One day, I asked Stretch why he stuck the arrow through Jack's head. Stretch looked at me with his usual poker-faced expression and said, "Because I couldn't stick it up his ass."

He said it with such conviction that I actually felt like it was a reasonable explanation at the time. Stretch would later be expelled from school for unzipping his pants and chasing the girls around the schoolyard with a crooked foot-long radiator hose stuck in his fly. He said he was Erection Man, sent from planet Prickton to please untamed schoolgirls.

Most of the guys at school thought it was pretty funny; the girls in the schoolyard didn't think so. Mrs. Stanger, the on-duty yard monitor, didn't think so either. She grabbed Stretch by his shirt collar and marched him straight up to the principal's office. The principal was shocked by Stretch's behavior and asked what motivated him to perform such a sick, depraved, degenerate act.

Stretch looked at the principal with his usual deadpan expression and said, "What's the problem? My dad chases my mom around the house like that all the time." Stretch was expelled from school the very same day.

Rubin and the rest of the group now approached. Nobody said a word. There were nine of us. None of us knew what to expect. None of us had ever done anything like this before. My stomach started to tighten as we began walking the few short blocks to the park. I tried my best to dismiss it, but the feeling persisted. As we walked, the confidence of the group gradually began to take over. Whatever we were about to face, we would soon face together.

As scared as I was, I was glad to be a part of it.

We eventually crossed Arsenal Street and made our way into the park. Our opposition was already there in numbers, waiting for us in a clearing in front of the trees. A couple of them had rocks in their hands. One had a knife.

My stomach tightened. The one I bashed with the trash can lid was there as well. He was staring right at me, but he wasn't carrying anything—at least not that I could see. He had a fat lip and a look on his face that let me know he was serious.

I tried to stay cool. I clenched my hand around the end of the bat and stared down my opponent. *Just wait. We'll see if you're still smilin' in about five seconds.*

We continued to walk toward each other. The tension mounted with every step. The reality of what was about to happen grew in intensity. Everything got real quiet. Then, all at once, all hell broke loose.

Rubin wrapped his arm up in his jacket and went after the guy with the knife. Rocks were thrown, and both groups converged in a spontaneous, explosive assault. I dropped the bat out of my jacket sleeve, caught the narrow grip, and charged my opponent. My opponent's face turned from serious to "holy shit!" He stopped dead in his tracks, turned, and took off. I was glad that he ran. I chased after him but not for long.

The chase ended when I heard the police sirens. I turned around to see what all the commotion was about. When I did, I couldn't believe what I was seeing. From out of nowhere, police cars were driving over the grass and into the park with blaring lights and sirens. They were converging on the group from every direction.

We scattered like cockroaches, running in different directions. Somebody must have heard about our encounter and called the police. We all met back up in our own respective neighborhood; and to my surprise, nobody was hurt and nobody got arrested.

There's a saying: You will never run faster than when the police are chasing you. I think that's probably true. Only one thing was different. In a matter of days, my name went from "Trash Man" to "Bat Man."

Our group disbanded shortly after. Everybody pretty much had their fill of Rubin. Out of nine of us, only three remained: Stretch, Rubin, and me. Rubin seemed unconcerned about the diminished numbers of the group.

Rubin asked out of the blue one day, "Where did the bat come from?"

I said, "It came from the bat store."

Rubin ignored the comment. He had another surprise for us. I showed no reaction. I had my fill of surprises.

———————

The next day, Rubin came knocking at my front door. When my mother went to answer, I slipped out the back door and ran across the yard, through the back gate into the alley. It was time to disappear.

I trotted up the alley and slipped around the corner, walking another block to Grand Avenue, where the buses ran. I didn't have any money, but I waited for the bus anyway. When I saw the bus coming, I walked to the curb at the back of the bus. I was waiting, pretending to cross the street. I wanted the bus driver to ignore me. As the bus came to a stop, I hopped the back bumper and held on to the advertising sign. When the bus took off, I was plastered on the back. The smell of diesel fuel filled my lungs as I watched the ground fly by in blurred patches of asphalt, concrete, parked cars, and pedestrians.

Four blocks later, the bus came to its next stop. I jumped off the back bumper and started to walk down the street. I was now a comfortable distance away from my house and Rubin. Whatever Rubin had in store was no longer a concern—out of sight, out of mind, as they sometimes say.

I walked about fifty feet when I felt someone grab my arm. It was a cop. He saw me hop the bus and followed me until I got off. He brought me home in a squad car and walked me from the squad car to my front door.

I'll never forget the look look on my mother's face when she opened the door and saw me standing there with a police officer. It was like someone drained all the life out of her face.

As she opened the screen door, the officer introduced himself and explained why he brought me home. His tone was polite and well mannered as he explained the obvious hazards of my irresponsible high risk activities. He finished his statement with a warning. "If your son is ever caught hopping the bus again, charges will be filed."

I told him not to worry—he'd never catch me again. My mother apologized for my smart remark and slapped me with intense disapproval. The cop laughed and said, "Have a nice day."

After the cop left, my mother grounded me for a month. To my surprise, she never said a word to my dad about the cop bringing me home—lucky for me. My dad would have punished me in a far more violent fashion. I was never so glad to be grounded in my life.

Rubin knocked on my front door looking for me the very next day. My mother went to the door, told him I was grounded, and that was that. She saved my ass and didn't even know it.

Chapter 4

Somehow, things were different. Life had dramatically changed. Bat Man became my new identity. I could walk down the street like a king, that's kind of how it felt. Being a king, however, is not without its own brand of problems. You see, when you think you're a king, you have to watch out for all the peasants in the world who think they're king material. This was my central problem. Believing you're something that you're not has a way of catching up to you. Every title has its price. I knew it wouldn't be long before I'd be challenged. What I didn't know was when, or where, the challenge would come from.

The challenge would come on a Saturday morning. My dad sent me to the corner confectionary to buy a pack of cigarettes. On my way back, I ran into Jack Mehoff. He was a grade ahead of me and a year older, and he didn't like that I was "in" with Rubin and Stretch. He wanted to knock me off my pedestal.

Jack was waiting for me with two of his friends, Jake and Mitch. As soon as I came out the door of the confectionary, I knew somethin' was up. I shouldered my dad's cigarettes under the sleeve of my T-shirt and prepared myself as best I could for what was about to happen.

Jack, Jake, and Mitch were leaning on a parked car, their eyes fixed on me. None of them said a word. As I approached, they sprang off the car as soon as we made eye contact. Intimidation was their intention. They blocked me from walking on the sidewalk.

Here we go, I thought. *How far will they take it?*

"Hey, Bat Man, I don't see you carryin' your bat today."

Jack was showing his confidence—and his rotten teeth. He didn't know it, but I was about to become his new dentist. My one step back must have looked like I was backing off. It was nothing more than a leverage step for a straight shot into those rotten teeth.

At first I thought I was facing another beat down. Three on one is a loser every time. But, surprisingly, the other two didn't jump in. I was shocked. The pack mentality was just the way it was. For whatever reason, Jake and Mitch left me alone. The fight was over before it started.

The old man was right: a quick take out. He knew what he was talking about. This reminds me of another rule I forgot to mention: If a beat down is unavoidable, do as much damage as possible. You've got nothin' to lose.

This was my first title defense. I was proud that I held my own. Some would say that I won the fight with a sucker punch. I didn't care. Jack should have thought about that before he challenged me. Besides, winning is everything when you consider the alternative.

From that day forward, everybody left me alone. At first I thought my successful title defense had something to do with it. I found out later that it had nothing to do with it. Rubin and Stretch found out about my unexpected three-on-one confrontation. I didn't know it, but Rubin and Stretch were waiting for an opportunity to set the record straight. Jack, Jake, and Mitch would soon pay for their attempted shakedown.

It took only a day for the three of them to screw up. Jack and his two accomplices didn't have sense enough to know that Rubin and Stretch would take exception to their shakedown practices. They made the mistake of standing together right outside the entrance to the men's room. The men's room was on the basement level at school, away from classrooms and teachers.

When the opportunity presented itself, Rubin and Stretch walked them down past a long row of urinals to the far corner of the room. All three were cornered against the back wall of the men's room. There was nowhere to go.

Rubin and Stretch were demonstrating their own special version of the intimidation game. Two other guys from the neighborhood, Mick and Sylvester, stood outside the entrance as lookouts to ensure that no pain-in-the ass teachers would interfere. No one was allowed in or out.

Jack, Jake, and Mitch were scared shitless. They didn't like being on the shit end of the stick. This wasn't going to be a pleasant experience.

Jake and Mitch tried to plead their case. Both emphatically stated that they never laid a hand on me. Their attempt to negotiate fell on deaf ears. They took part in it, and they were going to pay—simple as that. Jack didn't make any excuses. He knew he fucked up.

They were all so scared, they didn't even try to fight back. No one was seriously hurt. If they would have been, I would have found out about it. News like that travels fast throughout the neighborhood.

Rubin and Stretch never mentioned a word about it, but word got out anyway. These kinds of things have a powerful influence within a small community. Rubin and Stretch sent a clear message to everyone at school and the neighborhood as well: Don't mess with Roman. After that, everyone thought I was untouchable.

Things calmed down—at least for me. Looking back, I'd have to say it was the calm before the storm. Rubin would soon become a participant in what would later be labeled in the neighborhood as the fight of the century. The most surprising thing about it was Rubin didn't start it.

The fight of the century revolved around a nickel pinball machine located in a corner confectionary called Sam and Stella's. Sam and Stella owned and operated a small mom-and-pop store at the corner of Fairview and Giles. It was right across the street from a grade school. Much of their business came from school kids who spent their lunch money on candy, ice cream, soda, and snacks. The pinball machine was a big hit with the kids, especially during lunch hour.

On this particular day, Rubin was playing the pinball machine and winning. He had extra games built up on the machine and was well on his way to winning more. One of the four people watching Rubin was a high school football player. He was anxious to play and started to grow impatient. He had to get back to school.

Rubin winning extra games was beginning to frustrate him. The hot-shot high schooler made the mistake of tilting the pinball machine on purpose. This bullying tactic put an end to Rubin's winning streak. Rubin reacted immediately. He grabbed hot shot by the throat.

Sam, the owner of the confectionary, saw the whole thing unfold. He told them both to take it outside. So they did. The football player was confident. He was bigger, stronger, older, and probably in better shape than Rubin. But there was one thing the football star didn't understand: Rubin knew how to fight.

They went at it toe-to-toe, right outside the front door of the confectionary. All the kids from the grade school who were in the schoolyard during lunch hour swarmed across the street surrounding the fight. A huge crowd had gathered. They were all rooting for Rubin.

As the fight progressed, you could see the football player's confidence start to diminish. The last thing he expected was to be in over his head. Rubin was doing a whole lot more than holding his own.

Rubin was one of us, and the crowd was letting him know it. Looking back, I believe it was the first time in his life that Rubin felt accepted. All that positive energy kept him energized and at the same time drained something vital out the football star.

The hot shot started to panic. He was throwing everything he had, but everything he had wasn't enough. It must have been a frightening position for him to be in. Rubin kept moving forward, striking often with relaxed precision and deadly accuracy. Rubin was relentless. He stood unaffected by the football star's lumbering attacks. We all watched as the hot-shot football star changed from confident and arrogant to rattled and defensive.

Rubin was like an attack dog. The fury of the crowd inspired him to continue. The football star met his match. He dropped his hands in futility and gave up.

Rubin was still angry. He told hot shot, "The fight's not over until you pay me for the pinball games you owe me."

The high school football player was humiliated. He reached in his pocket and paid Rubin the money for the pinball games. The grade school kids all cheered. Rubin was the pride of the neighborhood—at least for a day.

This was about the time my dad started getting sick. He was still going to work, still drinking, and still smoking his unfiltered Camels. He started having more and more coughing spells. He would cover his mouth with a towel and cough. When he was finished, the towel would be stained with blood.

He finally went to the doctor, who immediately sent him to the hospital for tests. The tests revealed stage-four lung cancer. The doctor said the cancer was spreading rapidly to other parts of his body. Nothing could be done short of pain management.

The doctor couldn't believe my dad was still working. He gave him three to four months to live at best. Dad received the news from the doctor on a Friday afternoon. He rested over the weekend and went to work on Monday. My mother was furious. She begged him to stay home.

He walked out the door, turned around, looked at her, and said, "What do you want me to do? Stay home and think about it all day?" Then he turned around, got in his car, and drove off to work.

He worked another six months before he had to quit his job. My mother took care of him as best she could, right to the very end.

We got financial support in the form of a cash donation from my dad's co-workers at the shipyards. Sometimes they would come by after work and visit. They always asked if there was any way they could help. My dad kindly refused their help, but I could see he really appreciated their efforts. In the end, they proved themselves to be true and loyal friends.

He never complained, and he never felt sorry for himself. Me and my brother would help him get to the bathroom when he could no longer do it on his own. He refused right to the very end to use painkillers or a bed pan.

My dad lasted nine months—five to six months longer than the doctor's prognosis. He died in his bed—at home, with his family by his side. After his death, my mother found a job and immediately went to work. And that was that.

CHAPTER 5

A dramatic change in my life had taken place. My dad was gone, and my mother was working as a sales clerk in the shoe department of a clothing store. Her job kept her on her feet all day. It left her exhausted in the evenings.

We were all trying to cope with my dad's death as best we could. It was uncharted water for all of us. I isolated myself from both her and my brother by moving into the basement. My mother thought it was my way of adjusting to my father's death; she was right. I was hurting, and being by myself gave me a place to adjust to a radically new and different family dynamic. I no longer had a father.

My older brother, Rocky, started to play the role of the dominant male figure in the house. I was irritated by the change in his demeanor. He wasn't my father, and I resented the authority he tried to assume. My reaction was to ignore him. It created a friction. My lack of acceptance widened a gap between us that would never be repaired. I didn't care. He just didn't get it.

Rocky could never in a million years fill my father's shoes—not as far as I was concerned. I stayed in the basement and avoided him as much as possible. After a period of time, he realized I wasn't buying what he was attempting to sell, and he eventually reverted back to being who he really was—my brother.

I was just starting to adjust to this new way of life, or so I thought, when something happened that forever changed my relationship with my mother.

I woke up early one morning and walked out the front door and down the porch steps to recover the rolled-up newspaper that was thrown in the bushes. Finding the paper was a daily ritual that had to be performed. Our paper boy seldom landed the paper on the front porch.

I retrieved the paper from the bushes and started up the front porch steps when I was met by my mother. She was leaving to go to work. She smiled and asked if I was just getting home. The fact that she didn't seem to care whether I had been out all night crushed me.

How could she be so unconcerned about me getting home at seven in the morning?

I told her I was out with friends to see if I could get a rise out of her, but she didn't take the bait. She said she didn't have time to talk—she had to get to work. I couldn't believe it! She didn't give a damn that I was out all night—even though I wasn't. At that moment, I realized I could go anywhere, anytime, and do anything I wanted with no repercussions.

This was the start of a brand new life—a life of no rules, no supervision, and no boundaries. This was not the life of my choosing. I felt like an orphan. No boundaries felt like I didn't belong anywhere. There was no one who cared where I was or what I was doing.

I felt hurt, unloved, and more alone than ever. I lived under a roof with a family that no longer felt like a family. It was an absentee life. I felt worthless. I was angry that no one really gave a shit.

If I pushed the boundaries, what repercussions would follow?

I started having trouble sleeping, so I started going on late-night walks. I spent many a night crying myself to sleep after I got home to a place that no longer felt like home.

There was no escape from these feelings of worthlessness and alienation. I didn't feel like I belonged anywhere. It left an emptiness inside that would stay for years to come. Nothing could fill the emptiness. Drugs, alcohol, and all forms of distraction were nothing more than bad company, nothing more than pathetic attempts to fill a deep inner discomfort.

The people I associated with at this time were not my friends. Like me, they were flawed characters going nowhere. Even when I was with them, I felt alone. In the end, it's just you and the emptiness . . . you and the darkness.

Freedom can be a scary place when you're a young kid. Being out late at night puts you in touch with people who thrive on all kinds of deviant depravity. Men with bad intentions would ask me if I wanted a ride. The police were also a threat. Seeing a young person walking the streets late at night was a suspicious activity that perked their interest. I ran away from all forms of confrontation. I turned it into a game. I called it run from the police and the perverts.

"Come with me and have a beer," the sickos would say as they followed me down the street in their car. I cut through gangways, backyards, and alleys to avoid their attention. I stayed out long enough to exhaust myself. Sleep was the eventual sought-after goal, but it didn't always go down that way.

My late-night activities started affecting my schoolwork. I did just enough to get by. I had no interest in school and felt more in touch with the kids who didn't attend. The only reason I stuck with it was I didn't want to be a burden to my mom. As mad as I was at her, I saw how hard her life had become, and I didn't want to make it harder by being a problem. At this point, it was the only thing that saved me from personal destruction.

I was slowly adjusting to a whole new way of life—the way of the cool rebel slacker, who was neither cool, confident, or well adjusted. But I played the role anyway. I wasn't good at anything but being slick, and thanks to my dad, I knew how to stay one step ahead of most situations where interaction had the potential to get ugly. I wasn't afraid of things getting ugly. The rules were the confidence-builder that defined who I was. They were the only rules I had.

I was slowly turning into my dad. It was the only form of self-respect I had left to hold on to. I respected him as a man, and emulating who he was gave me a focus that kept it together after his passing.

As much as I disliked going to school, I had the respect of my peers. At least I had that goin' for me. Slowly, I adapted to this new, directionless, pseudo-independent way of life. I was the carefree rambler, too cool to care about anything or anybody. It was a comfortable identity to hide behind. I was a casual observer—a nonparticipant in the game of life.

I deluded myself into believing I had mastery over all of it, but deep down I was running on empty. This was all nothing more than a game, and I convinced myself that not playing was the only way to win. When you escape from life, all you get is regret. But that was a lesson I was still in the process of learning.

The only thing I eventually committed to was my friends. We were the fish out of water, and we knew it. But running with them offered no sense of resolution. They were all painful reminders that I was going nowhere, and my interactions with them ended up as predictable, bothersome, or flat-out boring.

Once again, I broke away. Not fitting in was starting to feel safe and comfortable. I was slowly adjusting to my newly invented identity and new way of life.

These changes weren't the only changes taking place. I was changing physically as well. My shoulders were starting to widen, and my muscularity naturally thickened. I was starting to mature—at least physically—and these changes affected my self-image in a positive way. I grew my hair longer than the norm at the time in a kind of punk-rock defiant tribute to being different without a reason. I was a typical teenager—too unconscious and inexperienced to realize I was no different than anybody else—but thinking that I was fueled my self-image. I was slowly rising out of the darkness, or so I thought.

I had a V-tapered physique, with a narrow waist and a flat stomach. My legs were naturally muscular, and their thickness accentuated the slimness of my waist. My hair was a thick dark-brown, and it laid longer to the left side of my face, partially covering deep-set dark-brown eyes—a trait I got from my grandfather, who looked like a dark-skinned, brown-haired version of Richard Boone. My skin was also dark in the summer; I tanned easily—a trait that came from my mother's side of the family. My mother claimed we had gypsy blood that came from relatives who could be traced to the Transylvanian mountains of Romania.

My wardrobe consisted of thin, worn-out T-shirts, faded jeans, high-top black canvas tennis shoes, and a chrome choker chain I wore as a makeshift belt held together by a small S-hook. I also wore a thin silver chain around my neck that held a silver medallion of the Dalai Lama sitting in a lotus posture. The inscription on the medallion read "Our enemies are our greatest teachers." I didn't know who he was or what it meant, but I thought it sounded cool.

I was starting to develop my own sense of character. As time passed, a new life was beginning to take hold. I was starting to carve out my own place in the world. Alone was starting to feel acceptable. I started to feel good about who I was. Gradually, life was starting to turn around. I wasn't what you would call popular, but I was respected. The hard times were over. I was about to enter a period in my life that would once again turn my world upside down, but in a good way—at least for a while.

CHAPTER 6

I was fourteen the first time I fell in love. Her name was Dianna, and we knew each other from a distance since first grade. We both grew up in the same neighborhood but hung out in different social circles. Dianna was quiet-natured, like many young girls who haven't quite figured out who they are. She lived in a neighborhood close to mine about five blocks away. Although we came from slightly different neighborhoods, we both went to the same grade school.

In eighth grade, we ended up in the same class. In the past, I had not paid much attention to her. But in that three-month period known as summer vacation, Dianna evolved into a trim, athletic, and curvaceous temptress—and she didn't even know it. She had an infectious smile and bright green eyes that knocked me out whenever she looked at me.

Every time I looked at her, I couldn't help but stare, but I never made an approach. Like her, I was still trying to figure out who I was. I lacked the confidence to break through that initial awkward barrier. I chose to keep my distance rather than fail in some awkward attempt to approach her and make a fool of myself.

One day, from out of nowhere, Dianna walked into the bowling alley where I sometimes hung out. It was the last place in the world I expected to run into her.

Grand Bowl was an old neighborhood bowling alley on the second floor of a large brick commercial building. It was a longtime fixture in South St. Louis, and it was within walking distance to my house. The place was poorly lit, with old, yellowed linoleum floors and an old-fashion hardwood bar with oversized leather and chrome bar stools. It had a signature odor of old wax, stale cigarettes, flat beer, and chlorine bleach that after years and years of neglect soaked its way deep into the very fabric of the building. The bar, the juke box, and six pool tables were the main features that made Grand Bowl popular.

The people who hung out there were not your traditional everyday nine-to-five Joe Schmoes. Most of them didn't have jobs, but they all had money. They were all players and characters of one sort or another who entertained themselves in a social atmosphere that had little tolerance for outsiders—bullshit artists and the like in hot pursuit of the golden goose.

Dianna walked in wearing an imitation-silk, leopard-skin mini-skirt with leather-frayed go-go boots. And I liked the way she chewed her gum. It was love at first sight—at least for me. But what I remember most is, as hard as she was trying to play the part, it just wasn't workin' for her. The attention that it brought scared her, rather than flattered her, and everybody in the place knew it. She was in over her head and didn't know how to handle it. At last, I found my opportunity.

Dianna was surrounded by three wise-asses who were entertaining themselves at the expense of her discomfort. One of them asked if she wanted to play pocket pool, and she didn't know what it meant. It was at this point that I stepped in and got her out of the place before she got the chance to find out. I ended up walking her home.

We struck up an immediate friendship. She liked the fact that I knew my way around. I liked the fact that she didn't. It made her laugh. We were getting more comfortable.

The topic of conversation moved on to my favorite singer at the time, Johnny Rivers: Was he a rock artist or a country artist? Dianna listened with great interest while I expounded my own highly specialized brand of bullshit about artistry and greatness and people ahead of their time who invent their own categories.

It was during that first walk home that I won her over. We just walked along together, real comfortable. We were like two old porch cats who shared the same space, drank in the same sunlight, and breathed the same air.

I was right in the middle of one of my passionate dissertations when it occurred to me that I was very much a part of the same element I was trying to protect her from. The truth of it stopped me dead in my tracks.

Dianna asked what was wrong as I searched for something to say—something smooth or witty or funny or clever—but nothing came. It was a moment of truth.

I felt like I was busted. So with a deep breath and great reservation, I told her straight up that I was every bit as big a problem as those three wise-asses I just rescued her from. What came after was this queasy awkward silence that oftentimes comes with its own daring brand of self-revelation, and that's when she kissed me. It was a kiss that changed my life, a reward from this beautiful green-eyed girl of thirteen for an honest and gutsy confession to a girl I hardly knew.

I didn't take it lightly and neither did she. We were inseparable not too long after, and it wasn't long before our relationship became an urgent quest for privacy.

Sometimes, unbeknownst to her parents, we would sneak into her basement and make out on the couch next to the furnace or slip into the back seat of her father's car when it was parked in the garage. And once we got trapped in the closet of her bedroom and had to stay there for over an hour when her mother unexpectedly came home. When we finally emerged from the closet, we both laughed at the shoe prints pressed deep into the back of her blouse.

These were the places where we truly found ourselves: in the dark-corner places of foggy windows, silent streets, queasy stomachs, and hot back seats; back-alley places where long, wet kisses ruled the dark, silent night and close conversations met the early-morning light.

There were unzipped zippers to too-tight pants and freight-train urges to an untamed dance. We hid in closets. We turned out lights. We covered windows. We lowered our voice. We made not a sound. If you caught us, we would die . . . just cravin' that magic . . . just one more time.

As I remember . . .

It was a late-night phone conversation that started it all. Our parents were asleep, and we were both talking soft to keep it that way. We were already way into the early hours of the morning, and the sneakiness of our conversation added excitement to the calm of early morning.

It was during a gap in conversation when the thought first came to mind. How strange these quiet moments: no words; no sound; no sense of smell, taste, or touch. And yet there's still some kind of connection taking place.

My words were soft and direct. "Ya know, it really would be nice if you could come over and just . . . slip your clothes off and climb in bed with me."

I had no idea she would actually do it.

My room was in the basement, away from everyone else who slept on the first floor. Dianna slipped in from the back basement door, quietly undressed, and slid under the covers. It was such a surprise, her warm, soft body curling up real close. And as I turned to face her, the feel of her presence and the softness of her mouth, her soft hair and sultry heat of her sex pulled me deeper as she bid me her welcome. I was in heaven. It was the most erotic moment of my life.

It was hard to stay silent. So much pleasure coming my way while my mother and brother slept on the floor just above. But the pleasure changed from earthquakes to a slow float on Sunday. We were porch cats again, basking in the silver-grey light that filtered through my only basement window.

We fell asleep soon after, as porch cats usually do, and I dreamt about castaways afloat in an ocean of emptiness. But consciousness came in the end and robbed me of my dream. But it really didn't matter, because once in a while—if you're lucky—you find one dream replaced by another. That's how I found her—naked and asleep, still in my bed, folded up right and tight, real close, her back molded to the contour of my body.

It was early, early morning, and I was wide awake and keenly alert to the soft light and cool breeze of a new day. I raised myself just high enough to catch the breeze on my chest and, leaning on one arm, I brushed the hair from her face and watched her as she slept. Everything I wanted was right there, breathing close against me, halfway under the covers.

She really was a beautiful sight, just lying there with one perfect leg protruding and then disappearing, oh so suggestively, under thin cotton sheets. I slipped one finger under the cover and slid it around the curve of her hips. The cover fell away. To look and not touch was unthinkable, so I stretched my hand across the small of her back and ran it carefully across those perfect, warm circles.

The slow drift motion of my touch was starting to arouse her. She was slowly starting to awaken, and the pleasure of her sigh—even though half asleep—stirred within me a great satisfaction. It was her lustful sensuality that I found so appealing. She was letting me know that she was all mine, and I wanted every bit, every last juicy drop.

We were lovers now, and it brought a whole new flavor to our lives: the luscious flavor of passion. How delicious!

"Good morning," was her greeting as she turned to face me on our first morning after. And we both laughed when she said it, for it was more than obvious that it was, without question, a very good morning. We were both so happy to be where we were—like kids who snuck off to Disneyland without their parents knowing they left the neighborhood. And once again, we danced the dance of the cat's romance while the neighborhood slept in the quiet hours of early morning.

"Is this the way to San Jose?" she whispered, as the ride neared the entrance to the tunnel of love.

"I don't know," was my reply. "But I get the feeling we're not in Kansas anymore."

———————

I was right. We weren't in Kansas anymore. Our morning was interrupted by the flashing lights of a police car parked in front of my house. We watched in horror through the basement window, but only for a moment, as a police officer exited his vehicle and started to approach my house. Alarm bells were screaming inside both of us. Both of us knew what the police were there for.

I turned to Dianna and said, "You need to go home!"

Dianna scrambled to get dressed and flew out the back basement door. When she got home, her mother and father were both waiting. At some point during the previous evening, her parents discovered that she was missing. Dianna's friends and acquaintances were called in an effort to find out her whereabouts. After many unsuccessful attempts to locate their daughter, the police were called.

Dianna had no other choice than to reveal where she had been that night and who she was with. She was forbidden to see me from that day forward.

I made many attempts to see her. But her parents put her under so much pressure that I soon became the problem I previously warned her about.

Dianna no longer wanted to see me. There was nothing for me to do but let her go. I was heartbroken.

My family dismissed the whole thing as puppy love. But I can tell you this: A broken heart doesn't know how old it is.

I felt helpless. It was another unexpected loss of someone I deeply cared about. The only person I really wanted, I couldn't have.

I tried to get over it. But sometimes, in sentimental moments, I'd find myself walking through empty city streets, looking for something that was no longer there. It was hopeless. It felt like another kind of death had taken place.

Dianna moved on to be a bright, attractive high school student while I was well on my way to becoming just another shit-bum high school dropout from the neighborhood.

Life went on, as they say, with both of us traveling the different paths of our own separate lives. But I never forgot how she made me feel: like someone . . . honorable.

CHAPTER 7

So time went by . . .

I eventually got a job in the shipyards as a welder's apprentice with the help of some of my dad's old friends. We made tugboats on the banks of the Mississippi River. The work was hard, hot, and dirty, but I was young and strong, and none of it bothered me.

Most everyone who worked there was just like me—uneducated, working-class locals who needed a job but couldn't find work anyplace else. A lot of the guys had prison records or other issues that made them unemployable, and for whatever reason, we all gravitated to a workplace that judged you by how hard you worked and not by the mistakes you made in your past. The unspoken rules were simple: Show up for work on time, do your job, and shut the fuck up. How hard is that?

Working on the river is really hot in the summer and really cold in the winter. In the winter, the wind coming off the river is ungodly harsh. It cuts right through your clothing, and the bitter cold seeps through your shoes when you're standing on cold metal deck-plate. In the summer, the heat from the sun combined with the heat from the cutting torches and welding arc fries you to a crisp under hot leather sleeves you wear to protect yourself.

Welding is a dirty job, especially in the summer. Once you start to sweat, the smoke, powder, and weld gases that burn off from the welding rods saturate you on every level. The taste and smell of metal permeates everything. Your clothes, your skin, your hair—everything is saturated. Even after a shower, you can still smell and taste the metallic flavor of slag. Black iron powder stains your handkerchief every time you blow your nose, and black phlegm stains your saliva when you cough or spit.

Most people turn their noses up at the idea of having to make a living with their hands, but there really is something truly beautiful about watching a luminescent pool of hot molten metal float across a cold piece of steel. It's almost hypnotic. The pay isn't bad either, but welders and laborers oftentimes have trouble holding on to their money. We got paid once a week—on Friday—and most of us drank up our paychecks over the weekend only to start the whole process over again on Monday.

There was a bar a few blocks down the street called Sparky's where we used to cash our paychecks. Sparky had a good thing going with his check-cashing service since most of the money he dished out for cashing payroll checks rebounded right back in beer and liquor sales.

I started drinking there before my nineteenth birthday. Although I was underage, I was never questioned. I looked like a welder, smelled like a welder, and kept company with welders and laborers who drank, talked about work, and bitched about everything in their world that didn't suit them. I was now one of them, and it suited me just fine.

Sometimes, however, the alcohol would drift my mind back to memories of Dianna. Our worlds couldn't possibly be more far apart. Hers was a world of cheerleading, new friendships, parties, after-school activities, a whole new and different social life, while mine was a world of hard labor, iron smoke, torch cutting, and heavy metal and iron fabrication.

Dianna mingled with clean-cut students who made fun of teachers and talked about who went out with who, while I kept company with hard-drinking laborers who worked their jobs, smoked their cigarettes, and told their dirty little stories. I convinced myself it was all for the best. No way would we ever fit into each other's lives anymore. Besides, I had no stomach for all that high school rah-rah shit anyway, but that didn't stop me from thinking about her.

So life went on, and so did I. Eventually, I got my own place—a one-room studio on the second floor of a building that provided plumbing supplies and bathroom fixtures to the local area. Having a steady job and a steady paycheck afforded me the luxury of being on my own.

To get to the entrance of my place, you had to walk through a gangway to the back of a two-story brick warehouse with a commercial store front. From there, it was up an iron fire escape to an iron-grate balcony that led to my studio.

It wasn't pretty, but it was private. And even though it was only one room, it was a pretty big space. The only thing I disliked about it was you had to walk through the closet to get to the bathroom. It was a small price to pay considering how cheap the rent was, and there were other features that made it impossible to pass up.

For example, the place came with an old white porcelain gas stove and a really old scratched up olive-green refrigerator. Both were left there by the previous occupants. They worked just fine. A rickety antique chest of drawers was also left behind. The open-and-close knobs were broke off of two of the drawers, but I didn't mind. I rearranged the drawers so the broken-knob drawers were staggered and left them partially open to make them easy to get into.

One of only two windows was located over the sink that overlooked a back alleyway used mostly for trash pickup and special deliveries to other commercial buildings on the street. The coolest feature about the place was the four-by-four skylight that provided natural lighting to the room. I found out later that the skylight was a scuttle hatch that allowed access to the roof.

Eventually, I bought an old painter's ladder and some aluminum lawn chairs. During the spring and fall, it proved to be a great place to relax, get away, and unwind. It was a wide-open space of privacy—my doorway to another dimension of solitude.

I didn't have a kitchen, but I didn't need one. There were old, faded, metal cabinets that supported a small sink and a pale-yellow Formica countertop that ran along the back wall. An exposed hot-water heater sat in the far corner. I had hot and cold running water and a place to store food.

All I needed to move in was a mattress, my clothes, some dishes, a coffee pot, a table, and a couple of chairs, and I was set. I borrowed a folding table and folding chairs, and bought the dishes and coffee pot at a second-hand re-sell-it shop, along with a mattress, sheets, towels, and various other odds and ends.

There was a light switch about six inches below shoulder level next to the entranceway door that was supposed to turn on an overhead light. You could flip on the switch once you made your way inside. But for some reason, the switch didn't work. So I bought a second-hand chrome lamp, set it on a stool next to the door, took the lampshade off, and plugged it into the wall outlet. Lighting problem solved. I was in business.

I loved coming home to my own place. I'd get off work, drive home, climb the iron balcony, and make my way inside. Once inside, off came those filthy clothes. It was hot shower time. From there, it was straight to the mattress on the floor until I got hungry.

I stocked my refrigerator with frozen pot pies, TV dinners, frozen pizza, and cold beer. I stocked my only cabinet under the sink with canned soup and canned chili. I ate TV dinners with no TV, but I didn't mind. The quiet atmosphere was a welcome alternative to the sound of cranes, grinders, hammers, air chisels, and diesel-engine heavy equipment that flooded my eardrums every day. I liked coming home to my "palace of solitude."

Eventually I grew tired of Sparky's. Sitting around with guys I worked with everyday, talkin' the same old shit, got to be a rut I no longer wanted any part of.

I took a hard look at my co-workers. The life they were living was really starting to take its toll—especially on the older ones. Smoking, drinking, and breathing toxic weld gases every day are not among the surgeon general's recommendations for a healthy life. It was time for a change.

I had just turned twenty-one and now had access to all the nightlife the city had to offer. My social life was no longer confined to Sparky's. I wanted a new and different life.

CHAPTER 8

I quit my job at the shipyards and found work as a bouncer in a nightclub called Shifty's. Shifty's was a bi-level bar with pool tables and a bar upstairs. It also had a lower-level bar with scattered tables around a dance floor and an elevated DJ stand. Disco was the popular music of the time. The people who frequented the place loved drinkin', dancin', shakin' their asses, and the social interaction that comes along with young people who are just starting to spread their wings.

When I applied for the job, Shifty hired me on the spot. I told him I had no previous experience. He said, "Neither did the last four guys I hired."

I couldn't help but wonder what that meant. I asked him how he got the name Shifty, but he wouldn't give me a straight answer.

My job was to check IDs at the door and watch the crowd to keep things from getting too far out of control. The idea was to stop a problem before it became one. There's nothing worse for the bar business than a fight. Physical force was always a last resort.

This was a job sent from heaven compared to working at the shipyards. I never got dirty or sweaty, I never got fatigued, and every beautiful woman who walked in had to pass by me. I couldn't believe I was getting paid to do a job like this: take IDs, watch the crowd, mop the floors, clean the bathrooms, and restock the bar at the end of the night. That was it!

I quickly got to know the bartenders, and before I knew it, I was part of a new and exciting social circle. Shifty's was becoming a very popular nightspot, and I was right in the middle of it.

Shifty's, however, was not without its trying moments. Trouble oftentimes develops around pool tables, especially when gambling is involved. That's where much of the trouble started. But trouble wasn't contained to just the pool tables. Anytime you mix gambling, women, alcohol, and drug use, you have the potential for a highly explosive cocktail. Twice I faced gunpoint situations, and that was within the first six months I worked there.

I was starting to question the motives behind my career choice. Easy money and chasing the ladies wasn't always working out to be what it was cracked up to be. I started to wonder what would happen if I got shot. *Who would pay the medical bills?* It wasn't like Shifty's offered extensive medical coverage. As a matter of fact, Shifty's didn't offer much of anything. Free drinks, a small paycheck, and a now-and-then cash bonus from the bartenders caught with their hands in the register, and that was about it.

Shot at Shifty's and shit out of luck! That was about the size of it. Maybe I'd get lucky and the bullet would kill me. Then there wouldn't be any medical bills. *But who would pay for a funeral?* Probably no one. Maybe I'd end up on a stainless-steel slab with a toe tag that read, "To whom it may concern: Here lies Bat Man. He died an honorable death—protecting Shifty's." How depressing.

I never drank at work even though at times like this, I really wanted to. Like the old man used to say, " Be aware. Be aware." It was good advice. I knew I had to stay sharp. It was important to stay focused.

I got good at reading people and spotting problems. Eventually, I grew to like working the early week nights, especially Mondays and Tuesdays. There were fewer people to contend with and less potential for trouble.

I remember one specific Tuesday night. It was very slow, which is no surprise for the bar business, mainly because the weekend doesn't officially kick off until Wednesday—which is "ladies' night," by the way. It was early in the evening, with just a few people at the bar who were calm in their demeanor and uncharacteristically unwound—an uneventful night working the door. That was fine with me.

I scanned the crowd out of habit and found nothing unusual —a couple of platinum-blonde, silicon-breasted beauties at the bar who were hot on the lookout for their next drink, their next drug, or the next dip-shit to provide either or both—nothing new there. I noticed the song playing in the background,

"Lookin' for Love in All the Wrong Places." *This could be a scene from a really bad movie.*

That's when I caught the movement of a figure in a low-light, far-off corner right behind the pool tables. It was the glow of his cigarette that caught my attention. He was off to himself, leaning against the wall with a beer in his hand. It was Eleven O'clock Alonzo. I gave him the nickname because he always got belligerent and had to be ejected at about eleven. He was already well on his way to another eleven o'clock departure.

I could throw him out right now, but why bother? "If you fuck with a fly on the ceiling—that's where you're at." That's what the old man used to say.

I was starting to get really depressed. What am I doing here anyway? Fucking with flies on the ceiling! That's what I was doing!

Once again, I took notice of the song playing in the background: "The Thrill Is Gone" by B.B. King. *I should shoot myself right now and get it over with.*

What I needed was a kill-time conversation, something to take my mind far away from this depressing set of circumstances. That's what I was looking for when, from out of nowhere, Dianna walked in. I was momentarily speechless. I couldn't believe she was standing right in front of me.

Dianna looked great. She was still trim and small-waisted in her own shapely sort of way. Dianna always had a kind of presence she couldn't hide. Her demeanor was always modest, and yet that low-key tribute to feminine sexuality always seemed to shine through.

She had on hip-hugger jeans and a pullover sweater. It concealed her figure but not completely. She smiled that killer smile, and as soon as our eyes met, we both instantly felt comfortable. It took only a microsecond for us to connect. It was something that just happened.

"You look like I feel" were the first words out of her mouth. She was smiling when she said it, and her comment made us both relax. We wrapped our arms around each other and hugged. The years instantly washed away. It was like we were suddenly transported to yesterday. How incredible is it that you can just know a person you haven't seen in years? It was surprising to me. After all that time, we still had the ability to connect at a level that ran deeper than verbal communication.

I always thought the moment would be awkward. But enough time had passed. We both found acceptance. We were friends again and were happy to be in each other's company.

She asked me how my life was going. I countered with, "Excuse me, what's your name again?" It made her laugh. In a heartbeat, we were back to old times.

We talked the night away, and right before closing, she said she wanted to dance. This was a first for us. We walked together downstairs to the dance floor. I reached for her hand and asked the DJ to put on a personal request.

It was late in the evening. The low-key rhythm of the music started to take effect. The song was slow, a soft, bluesy version of "My One and Only Love." The trumpet player was right on top of it, playin' soft, subtle changes off the melody and givin' the song a feel that was all his. I slowly wrapped my arms around her, and the both of us disappeared into the music. We were both different people now, but the chemistry was still alive.

I eventually broke the silence and asked about her life. I wanted to know if she was OK. That's when she told me her divorce was final. I heard from neighborhood sources that she got married. I didn't know what to say, so I didn't say anything. It just felt good to hold her and be close once again. So with the lights down low and the music real slow . . .

We danced the dance

of the cats' romance.

The leopards growled,

the wolves howled,

and Zorro dropped his mask—

for her . . . the love of his life.

Better make it last, I thought as I walked her to her car and watched her slip away into the night. And like a footprint in the ocean, she disappeared out of my life.

I went home and tried to fall asleep, but I couldn't.

What does all this mean? It doesn't mean a damn thing! Just one more thing to drive yourself crazy. Just let it go and move on with your life.

That's what I told myself. It was good advice. But I couldn't sleep. I got up, got dressed, and went back downstairs. Time for a late-night run. There's something about a late-night drive that clears your head. That's what I needed. I got back in my car and drove off into the night.

The sky was clear, the night breeze was warm, and it felt good to be driving with no particular destination in mind. I stopped at a late-night package liquor store and bought a bottle of Crown Royal. I went back to my car, cracked open the bottle, and proceeded onward. It was time for a much-needed, long-overdue, late-night excursion. It felt good to do something spontaneous for a change—like the right move at the right time, as they sometimes say.

So what the hell? This beats the shit out of lying in bed and star-ing at the ceiling any day of the week.

I raised the bottle to my lips and took my first drink. Nectar of the gods. That's what a welder would say. That's what the old man used to say.

There was a fresh smell in the air. It smelled clean and uncon-taminated. I looked out into the night sky, and the peace of the darkness relaxed me. The Crown Royal warmed me from the inside out. I turned on the radio. It was Johnny Rivers singing "Baby I Need Your Lovin." I couldn't believe it! The song brought me right back to the first time I walked Dianna home. I hadn't heard the song in years, and now—from out of nowhere—the song showed up just as unexpectedly as she did.

I turned the radio off immediately. It was like the powers that be were messin' with me. *What's this all about?*

I turned the radio back on again and started to laugh. Nobody would believe this—not in a million years. It was just too bizarre. *What does it all mean? Probably nothing.*

Whatever it was, it kept my mind engaged in the history of my life. *Am I being chased by the past? Is it some kind of sign or signal to pay attention to?* Whatever it was, it was way beyond my understanding. There seemed to be no escape. I finally brushed it off as coincidence. But still, it left an impression. It was really late, the Crown Royal went down smooth, and the warm glow of alcohol was starting to saturate me on every level.

There were almost no cars on the road. The smooth hum of the engine filled the soundless, empty void of a warm and pleasant summer night. I was floating on the slow current of alcohol and long-forgotten memories.

And slowly I slide . . . into memories reside. . . . My thoughts have survived! *Where will these thoughts take me?*

I really didn't know. . . . It just felt good to be out there . . . on the road . . . going nowhere fast . . . Going nowhere fast was right up my alley.

CHAPTER 9

Icruised down the highway for quite some time, drinking my Crown and enjoying the warm feel of the evening. It was a beautiful night. My car was running smooth, and the warm summer breeze put me in a good place. I was relaxed and in good spirits.

Seeing Dianna again brought me back to where I came from. I really hadn't moved very far. So many people have dreams and aspirations. I wasn't one of them.

I continued to sip my Crown and contemplate my life. *Where to go from here?* There was nowhere to go. I was a nobody in a world of somebodies—lost in a life with no purpose. Maybe that's what Dianna saw. Maybe that was the problem all along. I was just another shit-bum from the neighborhood.

Oil and water don't mix. Everybody knows that! Why can't I just accept it?

I wondered what my dad would have to say. *Did he ever feel the same way? What advice would he offer? We never talked about life or purpose or meaning. We never got the chance to have those kinds of conversations.*

What would he have said? … "Eat your cornflakes and shut the fuck up"—that's what he would have said. Maybe he was right. Maybe I shouldn't think about such things.

Eventually, I came to a bridge. I found myself crossing the Mississippi River into the state of Illinois. The fog of the alcohol was starting to take effect. I was about to enter the "East Side."

The East Side was an area where nightlife flourished. Many nightlife people from the St. Louis area found themselves crossing the bridge to the Illinois side of the river when they wanted to continue the party after the bars and nightclubs closed in St. Louis.

The East Side was wide open compared to St. Louis. All-night bars, strip clubs, dance halls, massage parlors, and underground gambling establishments were in full operation. This was well before gambling and casinos were legal. You could find pretty much anything you wanted if you knew where to go. And you could find a whole lot of what you didn't want, if you didn't.

People often joked that you didn't have to go looking for trouble in East St. Louis. Trouble would come looking for you. It was known to be a city were "whitey" was as welcome as a goldfish in a piranha pool. I ignored all the warnings. All I was looking for was a good time.

I found myself parked in a gravel parking lot of a night club that had a back door casino. The club was called Racy Lacie's Back Door. Lacie's was open for business twenty-four hours a day, seven days a week. If you had the money at Lacie's, you could buy almost anything you wanted. Sex, drugs, and alcohol were all readily available on the premises. If, however, you were caught doing any of the three anywhere near their establishment, you were promptly arrested and hauled off to jail. The rule was simple: Buy anything you want; just don't be stupid enough to get caught doing it anywhere near the place.

Many times I watched some poor unsuspecting fool buy alcohol, open the bottle in the parking lot, and start drinking right there. They were arrested on the spot. That's the way it goes for the dim-witted and unconscious. The thinning of the herd—that's how the old man would explain it.

At this point, I felt like blackjack was the answer to all my problems. Forget about all this philosophical bullshit. "Shut the fuck up, eat your cornflakes . . . and play some blackjack." Maybe the old man was right. Maybe that was the answer to everything.

I screwed the cap back on my bottle of Crown and slid the bottle under the seat. I had been here many times before and was starting to feel comfortable. They had good security. Many of the local police worked there to make sure the illegal operation ran smoothly.

I walked through the crowd, past the main stage and down a hallway to a door where a uniformed officer stood. Lacie's was jumpin'. As I approached the doorway, the officer opened the back door to the gaming room entrance. He checked my ID and let me pass.

"Good luck," he said as I passed through the doorway.

"Luck would be a welcome change of pace," I said as I entered the gaming area. My mind drifted off. It was time to check out the room.

The place was packed: slot machines, poker tables, blackjack tables, roulette, and craps were all fully loaded with patrons seduced by the temptation of fast, easy money. The tables were full, the smoke was thick, and the alcohol was flowing. The atmosphere was pure excitement. All my previous concerns vanished.

I found a seat open at a blackjack table and sat down. I laid five twenties on the table and slid them to the dealer. He spread the money across the felt of the table, counted my hundred, and gave me one hundred dollars in chips. It was a ten-dollar-minimum table.

The dealer shuffled and dealt a two-deck game. He shuffled fast, and he dealt the cards fast. I was enjoying myself. I played for about thirty minutes going back and forth in an up-and-down game with the dealer. My hundred dollar stack grew and shrank as the game progressed.

Most of the other players at the table were losing, with some getting up and leaving only to be replaced by others who were eager to get in the game. I was glad to be holdin' my own. I ordered another Crown on the rocks from one of the hostesses and settled back into the game.

The hostesses at Lacie's were beautiful. That's what this place was famous for. They were all dressed in revealing outfits—tight black-silk mini-skirts with thin, revealing black-lace underwear and low-cut lace halter tops that left little to the imagination. Distraction always works to the house's advantage.

Everything about this place encouraged you to go for it. They wanted you to lose control. That was the whole idea. Turn on the juice, squeeze every last dollar out of you, and send you home broke. That was their intention. I learned this lesson the hard way many times before. I was no stranger to losing, but this night was different.

After another thirty minutes or so of going back and forth with the dealer, I started winning. I was doubling on tens and elevens, and the dealer was starting to break. I found myself up one hundred and twenty dollars. It was time to make a move.

I took the twenty back and slid the hundred-dollar stack into the betting circle. "Black out!" the dealer called to the pit boss. He was letting the pit know that a big bet was on the table.

The dealer dealt the cards. He threw me a five and a nine—fourteen—not a good hand. After the cards were dealt, the dealer flipped over his up card—a jack. When my turn came around, I took another card. It was a five. I waved off the dealer and stood on a nineteen. The dealer flipped over his hole card. It was a three—for a total of thirteen. He took another card and broke with a ten. I was up another hundred.

I pulled the hundred dollar win off the table and let my original hundred ride once again. This time the dealer threw me a queen and a king for a two-ten-twenty. I waved the dealer off and stood on the twenty. The dealer drew to an eighteen. I was up another hundred. I was on a roll. . . . How far to push it? That's the million-dollar question every gambler asks himself. Knowing the answer to that one question is the difference between the winners and losers.

I let my hundred-dollar bet ride five times in a row, taking the hundred-dollar win off the table each time. I was up six hundred dollars. The pit boss was starting to watch the table with great interest. His eyes focused on the game with unflinching intensity.

I took five hundred of my six-hundred-dollar win and slid it into the betting circle. I had never placed a bet this big before. It was a really stupid move, but I wasn't worried. I was playing on their money. Still, I didn't want to give it back.

"Blackout," the dealer yelled to the pit. Once again he started the automatic process of dealing the cards. All the players, the pit, and the bystanders close to the table were closely watching the action.

My first card was a queen. My eyes were fixed on the dealer's hands as he started to lay down the players' second cards. When the dealer finally got around to my hand, he threw me an ace. Ace, queen, blackjack!

The blackjack paid three-to-two. My five-hundred-dollar bet paid seven hundred and fifty dollars. It was a seven-hundred-and-fifty-dollar win on one hand!

I was now up thirteen hundred and fifty dollars! I tossed the dealer two green chips and cashed out thirteen hundred up.

Most gamblers would ride a streak like this for as long as possible, but I didn't want to push. This was my biggest win in a streak that had far more losses than wins. I was happy to get some of my money back. I colored up my chips, took the money, and walked away.

It was time to go. I cashed out, put the money in my wallet, and shoved the wallet deep into my back pocket—taking great care to watch out for any potential threat as I proceeded to the front door.

On my way out, one of the exotic dancers nuzzled up close and whispered in my ear, "Want to party?" I knew she was sent over by the house to keep their money in play in the building. I responded with a polite "no thank you." She called me a tight-ass prick as I was leaving. Her smart-ass comment didn't bother me. I was leaving with thirteen hundred dollars of their money in my pocket. You have to feel good about that.

CHAPTER 10

There's a saying: Nothing good happens in East St. Louis after dark. In the first place, there are no saints in East St. Louis. It's just too damn dangerous. Many of the late-night crossovers from the Missouri side of the river are oftentimes drunk when they get there. Intoxicated patrons with money in their pockets often attract lowlifes who want to take it from them. Anybody with any common sense knows to stay away, but that doesn't stop everyone—and it didn't stop me.

I knew I was in dangerous territory. When I walked to my car, I looked around carefully before unlocking my car door, taking great care to ensure I wasn't being followed. I started the car, drove off, and started to relax. It was a painless getaway. I remembered the bottle of Crown stashed under the seat. With one hand on the wheel, I reached under the seat and retrieved the bottle from the floorboard. I unscrewed the cap and took a victory drink. Nectar of the gods. The old man would be proud.

It felt good to be cruising down the highway, heading toward home. I was on cloud nine, with the warm feeling of alcohol and victory glowing inside. I thought about how depressed I was earlier in the evening. It was like I now held the key to the universe: Show up for work on time, do your job, eat your cornflakes, play some blackjack, and shut the fuck up. This was the answer I was searching for. The old man was right about everything. I was Buddha, cruisin' down the highway.

As I crossed the river, I looked at my gas gauge and realized I was close to empty. Being back on the Missouri side of the river, back in home territory, put me at ease. I pulled off the highway and into the parking lot of an all-night gas station-convenience store.

After paying the attendant, I filled up my car. I realized I hadn't eaten. Barbecue potato chips seemed like a good idea—something salty to soak up the excess alcohol. I went back in, bought a bag from the all-night attendant, and walked back to my car. Time to go home and get some sleep. It was late, and I had to work the next day.

As I reached for the door handle, I felt a heavy blow to the back of my head. It rocked me to the core. A sharp pain shot through my head. The shock almost buckled my knees. An unsteady dizziness suddenly came upon me. My equilibrium faltered. I turned quickly and received another blow to the forehead. Blood was now pouring into my eyes. Both head shots almost turned the lights out.

I knew there were two, but I only got a good look at one. He had slicked-back blonde hair and a deeply pitted face. He was muscular by nature and had an oriental dragon tattoo on the inside of his inner right forearm. In that same hand was a crowbar that he swung with great accuracy, striking my head and shoulders numerous times.

I was doing my best to fight back when the crucial blow came from the other attacker. It was a blow to the knee from a tire iron. Sharp, intense pain shot through my knee as my leg collapsed. I fell to the concrete immediately.

All I saw of Blondie's accomplice was his worn-out, beat-to-shit black leather construction boots. I curled up in a ball and covered my head, shielding myself with my hands and forearms, while they continued to swing away. There was nothing I could do but lay there and take it. I was no match for crowbars and tire irons.

Repeated continuous head shots soon brought me to a state of borderline unconsciousness. The lights dimmed and then went out. My last memory was of one of them kicking me in the ribs and calling me a fuckin' pussy. He was wearing biker colors on the back of a shredded denim sleeveless vest. His jeans were dirty, and his brown leather cowboy boots were pointed. The patch on his back said the One-Eyed Jacks, Midwest Chapter.

* * *

I woke up from a coma three days later in a hospital intensive-care unit. I would later find out from the doctor that I had a severe concussion and dozens of stitches from numerous lacerations in a wide variety of areas. There were sixty-three stitches in all—twenty-two on my face and along my hairline, six on my right hand, seventeen on my right forearm, eight on my left forearm, and ten on the back of my left shoulder. I also had a hairline skull fracture from the multiple head blows I sustained, along with a cracked rib, loose teeth, and multiple contusions and abrasions from the beating I had taken. The doctor told me later that I was lucky to be alive.

"Luck," I told him, "had nothing to do with it."

I laid there motionless, taped, and bandaged, slipping in and out of consciousness with a headache so severe it felt like an ax had been buried in the center of my forehead. I would later find out from the police that I was fished out of a dumpster.

Apparently, I was thrown in the dumpster after being robbed and beaten unconscious. The all-night gas station attendant saw me being thrown into the dumpster and called the police. I would later go and thank him for saving my life.

At some point, the police arrived and asked if I remembered anything about the attack. I told them I remembered nothing, even though I did. The officers sensed my deception and warned me about taking matters into my own hands. I reassured them that I had no such intentions. After you've been robbed and beaten to within an inch of your life, revenge is the last thing on your mind.

They followed up by asking if I had any idea who could be responsible. My first thought was that someone from the East side followed me to the Missouri side of the river. It was a reasonable possibility, but there was no way to be sure. Again, I said nothing to the police regarding what I remembered, and I made sure not to mention the One-Eyed Jacks. I knew their reputation. There were consequences for getting tangled up with those guys, and I had already had more than my fill.

The police were eventually satisfied with my responses and went on their way. The who, how, and why of it would go unanswered—at least for the moment.

I found myself completely immobilized, though not by choice, in a hospital that was still as yet unknown to me. With nothing to do but think, I started to feel sorry for myself. Being alone never bothered me before, but the loneliness and isolation I now felt was starting to wear on me.

It was right about then that the memory seeped in. Vague—yes, clouded—absolutely, but nevertheless, it was there. It was the faintest smell of her perfume. I would recognize that scent anywhere. It was the second favorite scent known to me. And as I laid there, slipping in and out of a dreamlike state, I remembered her whisper, a soft, inaudible sound—not even a clear memory—and soft, delicate fingers caressing my arms, face, and hands . . . and her kiss moving softly across my cheek, chin, and lower lip. The clouded haze was starting to clear, and as it did, I wondered if Dianna had really been there or if it was all just a murky dream.

In spite of my limited mobility, my eyes strained as I searched and scoured my immediate surroundings. I was looking for a clue, just a tell-tale sign of any kind, to determine if Dianna had actually come to see me.

I resigned myself to the probability that these clouded memories were hallucinations—remnants of alcohol-induced recollections and sentimental memories of the past, that's all it was. That's what I told myself.

I started to question my sanity. *Was I dreaming this up? Can your imagination trick you into thinking you experienced something that never happened? Did the severe head shots damage my brain in some way? After all, I smelled her perfume!*

Maybe I've been damaged in a manner far worse than the doctors are telling me. Will I ever be released from the hospital? Will I spend the rest of my life institutionalized, being spoon-fed tapioca by big-boned nurses with hairy arms, female mustaches, bad breath, and body odor? Will I end up as a wasted vegetable, pissing through a plastic tube into a colostomy bag, singing mindless nursery rhymes to imaginary visitors, and drooling all over myself?

These were the questions running through my mind when something visual distracted me. It was the bright splash of yellow to my far left that caught my attention. A daisy, Dianna's favorite flower, placed in—of all things—a plastic urinal dispenser. I laughed at the sight and closed my eyes as my breath released the tension of wondering. It wasn't a dream. I wasn't going crazy. Dianna really had been there.

CHAPTER 11

Another six days would pass before I was released from the hospital. I went home weak and wobbly, but I left in good spirits—not in great shape but not too badly shaken either.

My plan was to try to find Dianna. Knowing that she came to see me made me eager to find her. And now that I was out of the hospital, I wasn't going to waste any time.

I took a cab back to my place and, once inside, threw my clothes off and started a shower—going about the business of cleaning myself up. After all, first impressions are important, and I didn't want mine to be a hospital smell. The water was warm, the soap smelled good, and for the first time in a long while, I felt really happy. It felt good to be home.

It was while washing my face that I first noticed the soreness and swelling, but I didn't actually see it until I went to the mirror to shave. Swollen cheeks, black-and-blue eyes, and a contorted jaw line. No way would I let Dianna see me like this. The sight of my reflection made me wonder what I looked like when Dianna came to see me in the hospital. *What did she think?*

Another three weeks would pass before I would finally look presentable, but the extra rest did a lot of good. When I first got out of the hospital, I looked somewhat gaunt and withered. Hospital food and fluid IVs have a way of doing that to a person. But all that was past. I was well rested, eating good food, and feeling much stronger.

As I buttoned my shirt, I noticed that I had put most of my weight back on. I was filling out my shirts again, and the snugness of their fit on my shoulders made me feel really good. I was back.

A light-blue button-down shirt was the order of the day, along with a pair of tight-fitted tan tapered slacks and brown-suede strollers. Clean and casual—that's what I wanted her to see. The canvas belt that slid through my belt loops notched farther back than usual. I lost some weight, but my clothes still fit well. I splashed on some cologne and was off to Dianna's parents' house to find out where she was living.

Walking up the steps to the house brought butterflies to my stomach. I was hoping enough time had passed that they no longer saw me as a threat to their daughter. I rang the bell and waited for what seemed like an eternity before someone came to the door. It was her mother. I always turned into such a bumbling idiot around her. It was easy to see why.

Her mother had the same penetrating, deep-green eyes that captivated you when she looked at you. Those incredible green eyes that made Dianna so attractive unnerved me when I came face-to-face with her mother. One look would reduce me to a mindless, incoherent nitwit. It was as if her eye contact somehow shut off the switch to my brain.

But this time, her smile put me at ease. I felt like she genuinely liked me. We spoke briefly about my being robbed. I could tell her mother sincerely felt bad for me. Eventually, I got around to the subject of Dianna's whereabouts. That's when I found out that Dianna moved to Chicago to live with a friend from college.

I tried to disguise the fact that I was let down by the news, but I couldn't fool her mother. Her effort to console me only embarrassed me. I walked away, embarrassed and uncomfortable, driving home with the same empty feeling I had after first losing her. And this is how it went with us . . .

Time and life would once again pass before unlocked memories would spontaneously resurface. . . .

As I remember . . . I was standing at the elevator in a crowded department store when someone passed by wearing the same perfume as Dianna's. It was as if the atmosphere itself was somehow altered by an unexpected dash of her presence. I was always skeptical when it came to love. I found myself surprised by my reaction. Tears came to my eyes. It was as if the scent had somehow transported me back to a time that long ago faded from memory.

It took a few moments for the rational side of my brain to kick in. I wondered if this experience was real or merely romantic awakenings of a past immortalized over time. I dismissed those feelings as adolescent emotions. *Hormones,* I thought. But still, I was grateful for the recollection. How strange are the forces of life and the circumstances of the universe.

I stopped at the elevator to contemplate yet another unusual coincidence when, from out of nowhere, fate hit me smack in the face. And as time seemed to stop with the click of the clock, the elevator door slid open and there she stood, stepping off the elevator of days gone by. It was Dianna.

The shock of running into her once again must have shown on my face. *This is just too crazy for words. How do these things happen?*

I couldn't believe it! After all this time! I was speechless. I thought for a moment about how over the top this chance encounter unfolded, but I didn't say anything.

At first it felt awkward—such an unexpected surprise, like that first kiss. And there we stood, holding hands in a formal greeting that lasted a little too long for a handshake. But the handshake grew to a hug, and the awkwardness washed away. We soon found ourselves having lunch, just two old friends enjoying an old familiarity, and yet there was more to it than that. There was always that special attraction. Both of us knew it. Both of us felt it. Both of us enjoyed it. But neither of us commented. It was a special intimacy that comes with old friendship. We always had a way between us, and it gave us great comfort—a certain graceful ease. And there was a kind of excitement between us as well. It was a way of making something as ordinary as a walk seem like an adventure, and off into the evening we would go.

More than eighteen months had passed since I was released from the hospital, and here we were again. I could still hardly believe this was happening.

Dianna looked incredible. She was obviously doing well. Her look from head to toe was classy, chic, elegant, and expensive. Beauty and intelligence are a hard combination to beat. Dianna had moved up in the world.

I filled her in on the details of my late-night confrontation, assault, and robbery that took place after our previous chance encounter, and as I did, I saw her concern. "How could this happen?" her expression seemed to say.

But as I spoke, I felt no outward sign of judgment or disapproval. Both of us had matured, and with it came a certain sense of knowing. It was an understanding that comes from the experience of living through many of life's trials and tribulations. The letdowns of the past had once again passed. And as we sat there, bathed in warm surges of flowing memories, the conversation took on a quality of self-declaration. It was a kind of striptease confession of the soul, you could say.

For in the space of an afternoon, each of us would soon learn the stark-naked truth of each other's inner-most thoughts and feelings. It was too powerful for words. And it all seemed to stem from the way that we looked at each other. It brought its own kind of smoldering warmth that burned deep down, like rich old brandy. And as we leaned across the table from each other now, hanging on to each other's every word, the intoxication of the moment, mixing playfully with the wine.

Was all this really happening?

The ocean of emotion was at work in this now-late afternoon. It was too late to turn back. Besides, who in their right mind would want to? Mind, for that matter, had nothing to do with it. So we forgot about the fact that we no longer fit into each other's lives, and we surrendered to the chemistry, the queasy stomachs, and the freight-train urges of the afternoon . . .

She brought me back to her place—the top floor penthouse of the Plaza Suite Hotel. The view was nothing short of spectacular—and the view out the window wasn't bad either! Dianna came out of the bathroom wearing nothing but a full-length, imitation leopard-skin coat. She walked to the side of the bed and dropped the coat to the floor. Then she stood for a moment and looked at me before slipping under the covers.

Not a word was spoken. And once again, we took each other to a moment ungoverned by rules—to a place that fit no notion of the old acceptable, a refuge where the wet smell of passion paved the way. So out of control! All old illusions died, replaced by passion's screaming song. . . . And love leaped in . . . like a leopard.

So for an afternoon, we both took a moment to step out of our lives, a moment to forget about the fact that neither of us fit into each other's world, a moment to rejoice, a moment to savor, a moment to remember, and then walk away. But that didn't make it hurt any less. On rare occasions, oil and water sometimes mix, but not for very long. And that's the way it went. . . .

Dianna disappeared from my life once again. I came to the conclusion that our chance encounter was a spontaneous, spur-of-the-moment rekindling of the past. As much as we were attracted to each other, this obviously wasn't going anywhere.

We were both different people now. We were no longer who we used to be. Our love for each other no longer fit our lives, so we both walked away. It was the hardest walk of my life. The finality of it hurt like hell.

Sometimes, as hard as it is to accept, painful goodbyes are necessary. Maybe I needed another shot in the head with a tire iron to get me back to thinking straight. Who was I kidding? Dianna lived in a completely different world. It was a world I knew nothing about. I needed to get my life back on track. It was time to let go of the past and get back to work, time to eat my cornflakes and shut the fuck up—easier said than done.

I couldn't go back to working at Shifty's. I pretty much had my fill of everything Shifty's had to offer. The job was just too tired. I didn't want to go back to the shipyards either. I was stuck.

Maybe a late-night car cruise would inspire a creative thought. I quickly dismissed the idea. My last late-night car cruise didn't end so well. I headed back to my place, parked the car, climbed the iron staircase, and retreated into my palace of solitude.

There's almost nothing that a time out and a cold beer couldn't fix. I laid on my mattress and stared at the ceiling. . . . I was depressed about Dianna. I went back to the fridge and got another beer—and then another and another and another and on and on—until?

The next morning, I woke up feeling tired, hungry, and hung over. My time out and cold beer turned into a twelve pack and a fifth of Dewar's white-label scotch. Still in the fog of the alcohol, I got up and a sudden feeling of nausea came over me. I ran to the sink and threw up—just barely made it.

That was close. This has got to stop.

A major world-class hangover was making its presence felt—not my first. *Never again!* It was a vow that was all too familiar—just an empty vow spoken in an empty room, talkin' to myself.

An unsteady, delirious walk guided me to the toilet. I had to piss. I unzipped my pants and looked down into the bowl. A cockroach was in the toilet. He was resting poolside on the dry edge of the porcelain. My stream knocked him into the water. I stopped pissing and watched him as he swam with great urgency back to the edge. As soon as he made it back to shore, I knocked him back in again. Again he scurried back to the edge. Once more I knocked him back to the center of the pool. The contest was on. He seemed to never get tired of swimming.

This went on for quite some time. It seems I invented a new game—piss on the roach. Eventually, I ran out of stream. After a long, arduous, hard-fought battle, I declared him the winner and flushed him down.

That cockroach was one hard-ass, tough, tenacious motherfucker. He probably didn't deserve to die like that. Who knows? Maybe he didn't. Maybe he made it back to his cockroach friends. If he did, he had one hell of a story to tell.

I washed up at the sink. The cold water on my face and hands was starting to bring me back to reality. I toweled off and slowly made my way out of the bathroom toward the refrigerator. It seemed like an endless walk to get there. As I opened it, I used the door to steady myself. The inside was almost empty—a reoccurring theme. A scuffed-up piece of paper laid in the middle of the top shelf. It was an advertisement for a pizza parlor opening in the area.

What the hell is that?

I picked up the paper and examined it. I didn't remember putting it there. I turned it over, and there it was: a verse scribbled in a sloppy, faded version of my handwriting on the blank side. It was etched out in pencil, almost illegible, like a child had written it. I had no memory of writing it.

> *Feeling lonely, feeling down,*
> *my heart in pieces on the ground.*
> *No more spirit, no more pain,*
> *nothing left to be explained.*
> *I crawled in bed and fell asleep.*
> *My mind shut down and ceased to weep.*
> *A bed, a grave—a lonely space*
> *to end this painful, lonely place.*
> *Bless me father, for I have sinned.*
> *My heart is gone. I cannot win.*

I've had enough of this shit. I tore the paper to bits and threw it in the trash can. *Where does this shit come from?*

CHAPTER 12

It was time to move on. No more feeling sorry for myself. It was time for a new direction. It was time to eat my . . . never mind. The thought of cornflakes made me wanna puke. My head was killing me. I needed food.

A quick scan of the refrigerator made me realize I had to eat out. *There's nothing here that's good for me.* There was a little side-street restaurant about a block and a half away, close enough to walk. I wanted food fast that wasn't fast-food.

I got dressed and made my way down the iron staircase, out the gangway, and on to the street. It felt good to be out of the studio. A mindless, fresh-air day with food as the only priority seemed right. It was the only *right* I could come up with in that moment.

I had no specific direction. Being out in the world with no particular agenda was direction enough. Distraction was the order of my life at the time. It was my only escape from depression. Something was truly missing. It was Dianna.

I walked the block and a half and made it to the entrance of Gert's Breakfast, Brunch, and Dinner Diner. Gert was a native of St. Louis who moved back home from Las Vegas, where she worked as a bartender on the strip.

Gert was a kind of comeback artist. She often gave unsolicited advice to her customers. It didn't happen every day, but it happened often enough to make me want to eat there.

Gert felt like it was her duty to help you see things clearly. Her advice usually came in the form of a one-liner. It was always unexpected and always a conversation-stopper. It was like waiting for lightning to strike. When it struck, it hit home with deadly accuracy. The shock value alone was pure entertainment.

The first time I heard her ambush a customer, I was sitting at the counter, listening to a guy complain about getting fired. He worked at a local bank and got caught bangin' one of his female co-workers in the bank vault. Another co-worker caught them in the act and reported them to their supervisor. They were both fired on the spot. The guy at the counter was mad at the co-worker who ratted them out.

Gert walked over, poured him another cup of coffee, looked him in the eye, and said, "Never let a piece-a-ass jeopardize your job." Then she walked away.

We were all speechless. I almost choked on my doughnut. I called her Gert the Guru from that day forward, and I've been a fan ever since.

Few people knew it, but Gert's real name was Barbara. Her ex-husband, Samuel, called her Gertrude whenever she got angry with him. Samuel fancied himself as a ladies' man, but that wasn't what he was. Gert described him as a degenerate deadbeat who had severe allergic reactions to work. She often referred to him as Sam the Sham because he was so full of shit.

Whenever Gert confronted Samuel with accusations of laziness, incompetence, or infidelity, he would counter with a question. "Who am I speaking to today?" he would ask. "Is this Gertrude or Mildred or Esther? Where's Barbara?"

Gert eventually came up with the right answer. "Barbara's down at the lawyer's office filing divorce papers."

Her response was more than just a joke. Gert dropped Sam *dead-nuts* on his ass—just like that—and never looked back.

I found an open seat at the counter and sat down. Gert recited my usual order: "three eggs over easy, a beef patty medium, rye toast, coffee, and a glazed doughnut."

"Gert, how do you remember things like that?"

"Mindless bullshit is my specialty, sweet pea." She always called me that.

She grabbed a clean coffee cup, put it on the counter, and poured my coffee. Her place was always busy, and today was no exception. I tried to sip my coffee, but it was really hot. I sat back and watched.

"Gert, how long have you been doing this?" After I asked, I wondered if she grew tired of people like me asking stupid questions.

"Longer than you've been alive, sweet pea."

Gert was small, trim, and petite—not an ounce of fat on her. She was older than me, but I couldn't help but wonder what she looked like with her clothes off. I took a shot of coffee and burned my mouth—instant payback for thinking that way. I turned my attention to the cash register.

Two guys were standing together, waiting to pay their checks. Both were anxious to leave. Suddenly, from out of nowhere, a hooded man with sunglasses stormed in the front entrance, pulled a pistol from under his sweatshirt, and shouted, "Everybody on the floor, now!"

The energy in the restaurant instantly changed. All activity came to a screeching halt as everybody dropped to the floor—everybody except Gert. Gert stood calmly watching as the gunman preceded to threaten her customers with a long-barreled version of a mini-cannon.

The gunman shouted, "Heads to the floor, and don't look at me if you want to live. Don't look at me!"

We all heard the loud click of the revolver as the gunman pulled back the trigger. He was letting us all know that he was serious.

The gunman ordered Gert to open the cash register—which she did. Without warning, he back-slapped her to the floor. "Stay on the floor like I told you," he said as he scanned the room once again.

He reached into the register and started grabbing cash. I could hear him stuffing it into his pockets all the while telling us to keep our heads down. I watched him from the corner of my eye as he reached down and snatched the wallets from the two customers at the cash register who didn't have sense enough to hide their money. After taking their wallets, he bolted for the door—stopping for just a second to put the wallets in his jacket pocket. That hesitation would prove itself to be the mistake that cost him his life.

When he turned his back to make his exit, Gert got up from the floor, reached under the counter, pulled a 32-caliber pistol from a hidden space underneath the register, and shot the gunman twice in the back.

The gunman turned to confront Gert. You could see by the look on his face that he was surprised that he actually got shot. He was surprised to see a one hundred pound waitress standing there pointing a gun at him.

He raised his pistol in an attempt to shoot back. Gert responded quickly. She put three more bullets in his chest before he got a shot off. He stumbled back five or six steps out the door, across the sidewalk, and fell backwards into the street between two parked cars.

All of us in the diner were in a state of shock. We all sat speechless as Gert walked calmly out of the diner to the spot where the gunman was now lying. With her pistol still in hand, Gert kicked the revolver out of the dead man's hand and retrieved the stolen money and wallets from his jacket. Gert would be known from that day forward as Mrs. Dirty Harry.

The police arrived shortly thereafter, along with ambulance personnel who pronounced the victim dead on the scene. We were all questioned and asked to give statements. The police finally released us after they took our statements. And Gert's Diner closed, never to open again.

I walked back home to my studio, poured myself a cold cup of coffee, and stretched out on the bed. Watching someone up close get shot and die right in front of you is an experience that leaves a powerful impression. Everything happened so fast, it seemed almost like a dream. I kept playing the events of the robbery and shooting over and over in my mind.

This was the second violent incident I experienced in a very short period of time, and one of those incidents damn near killed me. Not to mention the two other gunpoint situations I faced in my first six months of employment at Shifty's. *What did it all mean?*

It was like a movie that kept running nonstop in my head. I could still smell the gunpowder and hear the cries of panic from the frightened customers when those gunshots unexpectedly fired off. I couldn't stop thinking about it. Was I a magnet for this kind of thing?

Having four close calls in a short amount of time is not a normal life experience. I began to question everything. A famous quote came to mind: Those who live by the sword, die by the sword. *Did this statement somehow apply to me? No way possible.*

I didn't believe in all that biblical nonsense, and yet I seemed to be right at the edge of catastrophe on four separate occasions! *Was this a coincidence?*

I thought about the gunman and his violent, unexpected demise. I was sure that if he knew it was his last day on earth, he would have planned it a little differently.

The gunman made a fatal mistake. He saw an opportunity to capitalize on the vulnerability of an older female. He saw Gert as an easy target. He probably never considered the possibility that *he* could become the target.

He didn't know that Gert grew up on a farm and was raised with firearms. He didn't know that she sometimes bragged to her customers about being a better shot than her two older brothers. He didn't know that she had a loaded pistol hidden under the counter next to the cash register. He didn't know she knew how to use it.

Before that day, nobody, including the gunman, took Gert seriously. None of us would ever make that mistake again. This incident would become a life-defining moment for me as well.

I thought once again about how gravely close I had come to getting shot at Shifty's. Twice I came close to the same fate as the gunman who died between those two parked cars. I was with my father when he passed away, but watching that guy take his last breath was nothing like my father's passing. I saw the fear and sheer panic in the gunman's eyes as he tried desperately to breathe. It was nothing like the movies.

The explosiveness of the moment was a moment of complete unpredictability. It was an anything-can-happen moment, and most of that *anything* wasn't very good.

Working at the shipyards was once again starting to look really attractive. So back to the shipyards I went—only this time, I did my job and kept to myself. No more after-work binge sessions at Sparky's with my co-workers. If I felt like drinking, I drank alone in my studio or up on the roof.

And that's the way it went for quite some time, day in and day out. Work your job, come home, eat, have a few beers, go to bed, and do it all over again the next day—over and over, day after day. I was being a good boy—staying out of trouble.

This was the life I adopted. *Maybe I should become a monk and join a monastery. Father Roman, the monastic. I don't think so.*

Life was passing me by. . . . What to do? I was slowly becoming my father. I was living a lifeless, spiritless walk through a mundane existence. I no longer wanted to shut the fuck up and eat my cornflakes. It wasn't a bad way to live, but I wanted more. Plodding through life interrupted only by work was no longer acceptable. I was too young to stay trapped in what was starting to feel like a major rut. I needed something new—someone or something that would once again make life interesting and exciting.

That's about the time I met Adriana. . . . Be careful what you wish for. . . .

CHAPTER 13

I met Adriana at the laundromat. It was just another day in the routine of every other day. I had just about finished and was getting my clothes together. As I was about to leave, Adriana asked if I could change a five-dollar bill. She was short of quarters, and the change machine was out of order. I didn't have the change, so I ran across the street to the gas station, bought a bag of pretzels, and broke a twenty. I gave her the money she needed, and she thanked me. That was the extent of our first encounter.

The next time I ran into her was again at the laundromat. This time, she ran out of fabric softener. She asked if she could use some of mine.

"Help yourself," I said as I returned to reading a discarded gossip magazine.

I was distracted, immersed in the lives of old-time, legendary movie stars. I was in movie-star dreamland, caught up in the glitter and glamour of the rich and famous of yesteryear.

I looked up to ask her a question and caught her looking at me. She was pouring detergent into the washing machine and quickly looked away.

"Hey," I said. "Brando or James Dean?" She looked puzzled, so I repeated the question. "Who do you like better—Marlon Brando or James Dean?" I held up the magazine I was reading.

"Oh, I don't know," she said. "I never really thought about it."

She went back to folding laundry. It gave me a chance to really look at her. She had on baggy sweat pants and a loose-fitting sweat shirt. Her thick black hair was pulled straight back, and it hung real heavy, past the middle of her shoulder blades. She wasn't wearing any makeup yet she still looked good. Her skin complexion was olive, and she was well on her way to a great tan. Her wide-set dark-brown eyes slanted slightly at the corners, giving her face an exotic Eurasian quality. She reminded me of a gypsy—like me.

"For me, it's Brando all the way," I continued. "I never understood the mystique behind James Dean. By the way, my name's Roman." I stood up and approached her to formally introduce myself. "Actually, it's Roland, but everybody calls me Roman."

"So which is it?" She suddenly seemed standoffish.

"It's actually Roland. My dad gave me the nickname Roman when I was a kid." I was somewhat surprised by her sudden coolness, so I went back to my chair and sat down.

"I'm Adriana," she finally said. She followed up with a question. "So why Brando?"

"Oh, I don't know. I think it's a charisma thing. For me, there's no comparison. Brando's just got it." Adriana nodded in agreement.

I wanted to lighten things up, so I did a really bad Humphrey Bogart impression. "So tell me . . . what's a nice girl like you doin' in a joint like this?"

Adriana smiled. "What makes you think I'm a nice girl?" She said it like the cat who just ate the canary. Her answer made me laugh. Adriana seemed to be enjoying herself. She continued folding laundry.

"I'm a very good judge of character," I said, now feeling a little more confident, "and I think that laundromat people are some of the most interesting people on the planet."

Adriana rolled her eyes and laughed. "Now I know you're full of shit."

"Maybe so, but I got you to laugh!"

Adriana was starting to let her guard down. "I don't know if you're a good judge of character, but I think you might very well be a character."

Game on! "I happen to know for a fact that character is the defining quality that separates those who *wish* they were interesting laundromat people from those who *truly are* interesting laundromat people." I was on a roll!

Adriana shot back, "Well, if it comes down to laundromat people, I think you just might be one of the most interesting laundromat people I've ever met."

"Now who's full of shit?" I quipped. My confidence was soaring.

We both laughed.

"Can I ask you another question from one interesting laundromat person to another?" It was time to take the dive and see if there was any water in the pool.

"Shoot."

I paused for a moment. "What do you think about sharing a bag of pretzels with a laundromat person?"

"Oh," she said, now laughing. "The last of the big spenders! I don't know if I can take a smooth talkin' *pickup artist* like yourself." Adriana had a big smile on her face. She looked great.

"I'll tell you what. Pretzels stick between my teeth. If you make it a bag of barbecue potato chips, you got a deal."

"Oh! . . . A woman after my own heart," I said, now laughing, "and spoken like a true laundromat connoisseur!" Adriana cracked up.

So that's how it started—the two of us sitting together in the Laundromat, sharing barbecue potato chips.

———

The conversation went smoothly in the beginning. I asked what she did, and she answered, "a little bit of everything." I thought her answer was a little ambiguous, but I didn't pursue it any further.

Adriana said she was living with her friend Crystal until she could get more financially on her feet. Crystal came to the Midwest from the West Coast to pursue an old boyfriend. The relationship didn't work out, and after several months, she found herself with no money and no place to live. Crystal lived on the street for a short time and eventually resorted to prostitution to support a heroin habit.

Crystal was now working as a massage therapist because, as Adriana said, it was safer than working the street, and it provided a lot more money than she could make doing a "straight job." Adriana went on to say that neither she nor Crystal trusted men.

This was not the conversation I expected.

My next question was a simple one. "If you don't trust men, what are you doing talking to me?" It was the wrong question to ask when you're trying to get to know an attractive female.

Adriana paused for a minute. I threw her a curve, and it caught her off balance. "You remind me of an alley cat," she finally said, "and I have a bad habit of picking up strays from time to time."

Great! I just stepped on my own . . . foot. I was starting to wonder where this whole thing was headed.

"I have one more question for you. Have you ever had your heart broken?"

"What kind of question is that?"

I crossed a line. I was getting too personal, but it was too late to turn back. I now had doubts about whether I could turn this conversation back around.

"Humor me. I'll tell you after you answer."

"No, I haven't had my heart broken."

"That's good to know. Then we have an understanding."

"What understanding is that?" Adriana looked suspicious. She was wondering where I was headed. I needed to think of something fast.

"I won't put my heart out there for someone who can't do the same. That means we have an understanding. So in the interest of maintaining a laundromat relationship, how about we meet sometime—maybe say, a hamburger place or a laundromat with vending machines. We can talk about the lives of the legendary and chow down on Milky Ways and Jujubes."

Adriana laughed and shook her head no. "I don't know you well enough. Milky Ways and Jujubes might lead to something more serious. I don't know if I'm ready for that." She continued folding her laundry.

Things seemed to be cooling off, but the door wasn't closed—not completely. The conversation was still interesting. I've taken leaps like this before. Usually, I land on my ass, but I wasn't quite ready to give up. *One more shot at the title before calling it quits.*

"OK. How about I take both you and Crystal out for dinner tonight? Crystal can be the chaperone!"

"What restaurant?"

"You choose. I'll leave it up to the two of you. Think of it as a free dinner for two at the laundromat of your choice." Adriana once again laughed.

"Pick us up at seven. That's when Crystal gets off."

"I'll see you tonight at seven. Where should I pick you up?"

"Pick us up where Crystal works. Do you know where Blue Skies Massage Parlor is, across the river?"

"Where?" This wasn't unfolding quite the way I expected.

"Blue Skies Massage Parlor. That's where Crystal works. Do you know where it is?" Adriana was closely watching my reaction. I tried to stay cool.

"Yes, I know where it is," I said—even though I didn't. "I'll see you tonight at seven."

"Don't be late. Crystal and I don't like to eat after eight."

Unbelievable! This is without question the strangest laundromat day of my life.

CHAPTER 14

I drove home and changed into grey dress slacks, a black cotton dress shirt, and black leather slip-ons. I wanted to be clean enough to look good without looking like I was trying too hard. I had some time to kill, so I lounged around for about two hours before I drove across the river to find Blue Skies.

It didn't surprise me that Adriana didn't want me picking her up where she lived. After all, I hardly knew her. What if I was an ax murderer? If I knew where she lived, I could return to her house and hack her to bits any time I felt like it—not a good arrangement for her. This arrangement probably made her feel a little more comfortable. Still, I wondered if she would show up. Maybe she was just pulling my chain. Maybe it was all a big joke.

When I got to Blue Skies, I was relieved to see Adriana waiting outside. What a transformation! She went from frumpy laundromat lady to alluring, mysterious gypsy woman! She had a million-dollar smile that lit up like fireworks. Her dark-brown Indian-like eyes had a depth that pulled you right in. Adriana had a face like a movie star. I tried to stay cool.

"Where's Crystal?" I asked.

"She's busy with a customer. She can't come."

Good! I thought to myself.

I opened the car door for her, and she jumped in the passenger seat. I got in and off we went. Concentrating on the road was a huge problem. Adriana looked every bit as exotic as her name.

Adriana wanted a steak from Aurie's Elite Gourmet Steak House. As we headed to our destination, I felt compelled to ask a question.

"So why did you agree to go out with me?"

"Because you were funny. I got a kick out of you. Even if you are full of shit, at least you're amusing. I never had so much fun in a laundromat! You also have a really nice ass."

"I can live with that."

"Did you have any problem getting here?" Adriana asked.

"No. . . It was easy to find."

I was distracted. My mind went back to seeing Adriana standing in front of Blue Skies. It was a visual contrast that couldn't be ignored. The scene reminded me of a surrealistic European art movie. A woman as attractive as Adriana had no business being in a place like that. It seemed odd.

Blue Skies was a four-story renovated grain silo that was converted to a commercial building. It was painted bright sky blue and had two shabbily installed picture windows on each side of the front door. Both windows were covered with vertical blinds that were kept closed. The small neon sign that hung in front of the blinds was not readable from passing cars that traveled along the highway. The sign read Blue Skies Massage Parlor, Where the Sky's the Limit.

I couldn't help but wonder, *was I somehow being tested?*

When we arrived at Aurie's, I walked around the car to open Adriana's door. When she got out of the car, I got another good look at her. She looked terrific, and I told her so. She had on a tight, black short skirt that flattered the contour of her figure and black stiletto heels that accentuated her calves. A thin platinum chain wrapped around her right ankle, and two twin-studded diamond earrings, one above the other, pierced her left ear. Adriana looked sexy and polished—almost elegant, even though she wasn't.

As we walked to the entrance of the restaurant, I couldn't help but notice her long, tanned legs that tied in quite well to a nice, well-rounded rear end. She had a subtle walk that really caught my attention. Her hips swayed back and forth to a rhythm all their own. Adriana really knew how to work it.

We were shown to a quiet, out-of-the-way table where we sat down and ordered drinks—a Black Russian on the rocks for me and a Bailey's Irish Cream on the rocks for Adriana. We ordered steaks with loaded baked potatoes and salads with Aurie's Elite house dressing.

After the waiter left, Adriana asked, "So how did you get those scars on your face?"

"It's kind of a long story. I'm not trying to be deceptive, but it's probably not a story you want to hear before you eat."

"So, who *are* you?" Adriana's look was very direct. She had questions and wanted answers.

For a second, I was startled by the directness of her question. I opened up and told her everything—where I worked and where I used to work, where I lived, and where I came from. I also talked about what I liked, what I didn't like, and what I liked about her. I told her about my friends, family, and some of the characters I knew and grew up with. I talked about growing up in the city and city life in general. I also revealed how much I liked and valued my privacy.

Adriana listened as I unveiled some of the history and mystery of my life. We ordered more drinks, and the conversation gravitated back to her.

"I ran away from home when I was fourteen, after my step-father made a move on me. I eventually hooked up with an older guy named Austin who took me in and said he'd take care of me. He was a motorcycle guy, and I was always attracted to bad boys. I was young and naive—looking for excitement. I ended up with crazy. I should have known better, but I ignored my instincts.

"As soon as I moved in, the relationship became volatile. Austin turned out to be a psychotic, out-of-control, alcoholic, drug addict, but I didn't see it right away. I was too busy living the fantasy of being a biker chick.

"Austin said he'd change my life, and he did. Every day, he dominated my life more and more. He held me in check with fear, intimidation, alcohol, and heroin.

"He knew I was in over my head, and he continued to pour it on. He started referring to me as his 'forever property.' At first, I thought it was a joke. I kept telling myself that things would get better, but they only got worse. I finally realized none of it was a joke. He really did regard me as his property.

"He actually gave me a dog collar with my name stamped on a chrome medallion. By then, I was so broke-down and intimidated, I was afraid not to wear it. I felt trapped. I knew if I left him, he'd come after me, but I left him anyway. I've been in hiding ever since."

I listened while Adriana continued.

"Austin is very cunning. He's like a viper that wraps himself around you before he sinks his teeth in. He never outwardly threatened me; he didn't need to. He knows I'm scared to death of him. He will cross every line and leave no stone unturned when it comes to getting even—especially if he thinks you've betrayed him. He hurts people for his own amusement, and he has no conscience about it. By leaving him, I've dishonored him, and for that there's a price to pay. . . . I don't want to find out what that price is."

Here we go. I should have known that a woman this attractive doesn't come without her own special version of trouble.

I sat back while Adriana continued her story.

"Austin's been in and out of prison his whole life. He's violent and sadistic, and he'll destroy anybody who crosses him. His weapon of choice is intimidation. He uses it all the time, and he's good at it. Every day I was with him was a day of fear and uncertainty—like living in my own private hell. I swore to myself after I left that I would never let anybody do that to me again."

Adriana paused for a moment and looked at me. "If you want to get up and run for the hills, I completely understand."

"Go ahead and finish. I'm not going anywhere."

Adriana continued. "You see, it's like this. I'm tired of this life, and I want a new one. I want a life that's free of shit-heads, losers, players, and psycho-lunatics. I'm looking for someone who has some measure of honesty, integrity, and stability. I won't settle for anything less."

Adriana settled back in her chair. She said everything she wanted to say. The ball was clearly in my court.

I sat there, trying to digest everything Adriana revealed. I had more questions about her past, but I chose not to go there. Adriana never went into great detail about her life before she met Austin or what she had to do to make a living, and I never brought it up. She never again mentioned the scars on my face, and I never offered an explanation. Some things are better off left alone.

I wondered at this point what I was getting myself into. Taking Adriana's advice seemed like a pretty reasonable idea. *Maybe I should get up and run for the hills.* But I didn't.

Adriana's straightforwardness and openness made me even more attracted to her. At this point, I didn't give a shit about Austin. I didn't care who he was or what he was capable of. I was ready to jump in with both feet. . . . So I did.

I looked at Adriana and told her straight up that I would never lie to her. I said that everything I revealed to her this evening about my history, my likes and dislikes, all of it was exactly the way it was.

"I haven't told you everything about myself," I said, "but I haven't hidden anything either. Beyond that, I don't know what else to say."

Adriana paused for a moment. She chose her words carefully. "You've been very truthful with me. Now I have to tell you, I haven't been totally honest with you."

Here we go, I thought. *Confession time.* I sat back and waited for another bomb to drop. "Say what you need to say."

"OK, so here it is. Crystal didn't really have to work. I just told you that so I could have you all to myself."

I was speechless. . . . Her directness and openness were incredible turn-ons. After taking a moment to gather myself, I said, "This really has been quite an evening. I don't think I've ever had a first date like this."

I searched her face in an effort to find out where this whole thing was headed. It felt like the subtle fire and flirtatiousness between us in the beginning was starting to burn really hot. If this evening was a test, so far I felt like I was passing.

The evening was starting to wind down, but the conversation wasn't. Adriana seemed as interested in me as I was in her. Things were moving fast, but I still wasn't sure what to make of it—so I didn't make anything of it. Never drop your pants before the woman drops hers. . . . Words to live by if you want to avoid making a fool of yourself.

The waiter appeared at our table and asked if we wanted dessert. We both declined. He handed me the check. I paid the waiter and sat back comfortably in my chair. I thought the evening was over, but I was wrong. Adriana had something else to reveal.

Adriana leaned into me before she spoke. "There's something else about me I think you need to know."

This sounded serious. I didn't know it, but she had me right where she wanted me. Like most men, I was about five steps behind.

"Really? What is it?"

"I'm a psychic," she said matter-of-factly. She took both my hands and wrapped her fingers into mine. She was now in charge. I was too enamored to notice.

"Tell me what you see." I leaned into her, waiting for her to respond. I was hooked, and she knew it.

"I can see into your future, and I can see that you are a very lucky man."

"Fascinating. How so?"

"I can see that in about forty-five minutes, that you are going to hit the *jackpot!*"

What a statement! I laughed out loud and said, "I think this could be a lottery win!" We both cracked up. Our chemistry was unbelievable. I was cruising at high altitude.

"Would you like another drink?" I asked.

"No, thank you," she said as she sipped the last of her drink. "I think it's time to go."

Adriana took my hand, and our fingers interlocked. *What a great night!*

Adriana didn't mince words. She had a face like an angel and a mouth like a truck driver. Everything about her was fast. She didn't waste time playing games. She made her decisions in the blink of an eye, and that was it. No time for bullshit, and no time for bullshitters. We were well on our way to an incredible connection. I wasn't sure where it was all going, but as first dates go, I felt like this was one for the record books. As we made our way to my car, I thought, *Don't screw this up!*

Generally, I say or do at least one stupid thing before the evening ends. But this night was different. I didn't say or do anything offensive, I didn't trip or fall, I didn't spill anything, and I didn't embarrass Adriana or myself in any way. The god of perfect first dates was smiling upon me—so far.

As I opened the passenger door, Adriana got in and said, "Take me to your place."

Jackpot!

Adriana stayed with me all night. It was truly an unforgettable evening all the way around. There's nothing more gratifying than waking up with a beautiful woman lying right next to you.

We didn't get up until late morning. We eventually got around to breakfast. After we ate, late morning turned into early afternoon. We were still having a great time. That's when I asked Adriana if she wanted to move in. I knew it was a gamble, but as far as gambles go, I felt like this was a gamble I couldn't lose. Fast, loose, and reckless—what the hell!

I helped Adriana pack up her things at Crystal's place and move into my studio early that evening.

It was later in the evening when Crystal arrived home to discover Adriana's note on the kitchen table:

Dear Crystal,

> I have bad news and good news.
> The bad news is, as you probably already
> know, I moved out while you were at work today.
> The good news is, I've got a new boyfriend.
> Thanks for being there for me. I'll stay in touch.
>   Love, Adriana

I told Adriana up front that she would have to get a job—and it would make more sense if it was on this side of the river. Adriana agreed and found a job within days as a salesgirl in the cosmetics section of a local pharmacy.

Adriana thought I'd be surprised that she landed a job so fast, but I wasn't surprised in the least. Attractive women never seem to have employment problems. It was like it was meant to be. It was a new start for both of us.

CHAPTER 15

So by and by,
the years went by.
No longer a bouncer,
no longer a spy,
no longer an agent for the FBI.
I was still a welder.

"And what does this have to do with the price of rice?" you ask.

Well, all I can say is, it may not have been a very exciting way of life, but it was a way of life that brought both of us peace.

Adriana was now working as a secretary. We were still living in my "palace of solitude," but Adriana insisted that we make some improvements.

The lamp on the stool next to the door had to go. We bought studio lights and suspended them from brackets I screwed into the ceiling. A chrome and Formica kitchen set, complete with four matching chrome chairs with red vinyl seat covers, was a new addition. We also purchased a stereo system and an entertainment center with a big-screen TV. We found another chest of drawers at a garage sale and bought an antique chifforobe to store most of my clothing. Adriana took over my closet about twenty minutes after she moved in, but I didn't mind. She seemed happy.

At first, I was concerned that my place wasn't good enough for her, but Adriana said she felt safe with me. I was glad she felt that way.

Later in the week, I had a brainstorm of an idea. I built a mattress frame out of two-inch angle iron at work during my lunch hour. After work, I brought the metal frame home, put the mattress inside, and suspended the frame and mattress from four chains anchored into the ceiling. The bed now swung from the corners like a porch swing. *Very cool indeed!*

In the beginning, nobody gave us a snowball's chance in hell of making it. After all, we hardly knew each other. But the everyday experience of living together led to discoveries that made life interesting. It brought us closer together.

We always had great conversations. They created an intimacy between us that deepened with time. Our best conversations seemed to take place late at night. There's something about a dark room or a wide-open, clear night sky that makes it easier to open up and bare your soul.

Neither of us knew why the relationship worked. It just did. We got along, there were no fights, and there was no drama. Both of us had our fill of riding the rollercoaster, and neither of us was interested in that kind of emotional joyride. It seemed like the better we got to know each other, the more we enjoyed each other's company. This was a rarity as far as most couples go.

We talked about marriage and children, but Adriana wanted no part of either one. She said life was hard enough without the responsibility of kids.

She was afraid that marriage might ruin the great thing we had together. I couldn't argue. My mom and dad were hardly a model for a happy life, and I didn't want to sabotage the two of us any more than she did.

———

Everything was going smoothly. I got off work earlier than her, so I could shower, clean up, and relax for a while before she came home. We spent our evenings together watching TV, going to movies, and eating out when we could afford it. We watched late-night movies, ate popcorn in bed, and binged out on chocolate milk and doughnuts every once in a while.

Adriana especially liked the rooftop. We spent many nights stretched out on lawn chairs, looking up at the night sky and enjoying the breezes of the evening when the weather was right.

Sunbathing on the rooftop was also one of Adriana's favorite pastimes. The rooftop provided both privacy and solitude when one of us wanted to be alone.

Music was also a part of everyday life. We both liked dance rhythms and the blues. The atmosphere in the studio was either quiet or musical. It was a special place to come home to.

Sometimes we barbecued on the rooftop. The smoke from the barbecue would filter its way down to the street. The customers from the ground level would often ask where the barbecue smell was coming from. It wasn't a smell they expected from a plumbing supply house.

Every once in a while I sent pork steaks and brats to the guys who worked downstairs behind the parts and supply counter. They always appreciated it. My relationship with them was good. They owned the building, and I always paid my rent on time. Everybody got along.

Living together unfolded smoothly. We were both quiet-natured, and it made living together in a studio apartment a whole lot easier. Both of us seemed to have a kind of intuition with each other. We always seemed to know when to leave each other alone.

I had my vision of the world, and Adriana had hers. They were almost never the same, but our differences didn't cause any serious friction. Adriana's differences were what made her interesting. Her presence always held my attention whether I agreed with her or not.

Adriana had a vibrancy that ran deeper than external beauty. When she spoke, her eyes reflected an understanding you couldn't take for granted.

Deep down, Adriana was fractured, but she still retained the ability to be who she was in spite of the scars she carried. I think she saw her beauty as a curse. Maybe that's why she picked me. I had scars as well—both inside and out. We were both flawed, twisted in some unnatural way by life. But with each other, we always kept the doors open. A natural honesty and spontaneity between us kept things moving.

Adriana was a player when she wanted to be, and she loved it when I called her on it. She used her beauty like a surgeon uses a scalpel. I watched her manipulate sales clerks, gas station attendants, police officers, and teenage boys—all of them hopelessly seduced into submission much like I was when we first met. They would run to the store for her, take out our trash, or carry her groceries. After each of her performances, I would applaud. "That was wonderful," I would say in my own dry, sarcastic way, and Adriana would laugh at the absurdity of it all.

She once said, "If you feed and fuck a man, you can own him for life." I told her she could eliminate 50 percent of that equation and still own him for life.

———

One night, after a late-night supper, we made love on the kitchen table. It was one of those early times in the relationship when we were still intensely engaged in the process of discovery. In seconds, plates and dishes were pushed aside, clothes were discarded, and it was on.

We were both wrapped up in the heat of the moment when Adriana suddenly grew quiet. "I smell vinegar," she said. Adriana looked bewildered.

All activity came to an abrupt halt. I was puzzled, to say the least. It was a strange thing for her to say under the circumstances. Then I noticed a shred of lettuce tangled in her hair. As I looked closer, I brushed her hair aside and broke out in laughter.

"What are you laughing at?" Adriana said.

"You got your head in the salad bowl."

We both laughed so hard that the table collapsed. We went crashing to the floor, which made us laugh even harder. It was but one of the special moments that defined our relationship.

On weekends when we were both off, I would sometimes make her breakfast. These were always special times as well. Adriana would sit at the table and keep me company while I kept myself occupied with light-hearted conversation, over-easy eggs, bacon, and cinnamon French toast.

I loved that I could still make her laugh. I wasn't the richest, the smartest, or the best-looking guy she ever met, but nobody would ever love her more than me. Neither of us made a lot of money, but between the two of us, we both carved out a life. We gave to each other what we had. You can't expect more than that.

My family accepted her immediately. Adriana felt included. But sometimes she worried about her shaky past. I understood her concern. My history was a rocky one as well. I told her not to worry. We both had our fair share of failures. It was time to move on. Adriana agreed. After all, this was the new life she was looking for—a new life filled with new possibilities. I did my best to try to give it to her.

Life overall became routine, but it was stable and comfortable—not a bad way to be. But what happens when the old life runs into the new life? . . . What happens then?

CHAPTER 16

Everything changed one day when Adriana received a hand-written letter in an unmarked envelope. It was taped to the outside of our door. Only the name Adriana was written on the envelope. There was no return address and no stamp. Somebody hand-delivered it to our door.

Adriana opened the envelope and unfolded the letter. There were only five words scribbled in capital letters with a magic marker: "I KNOW WHERE YOU LIVE." As Adriana handed me the letter, her hand started to tremble.

"Austin found me."

I didn't know what to say. I was angry, but I didn't want to show it. I resented the threat and intrusion on our life, but I didn't want to add any more tension to the situation. I wanted to reassure her that everything would be alright, but I couldn't find it within myself to say anything.

Eventually, Adriana started to calm down. It gave me the chance to ask about her former boyfriend, Austin.

"Tell me everything you can think of about him. Describe him to me. No detail is too small."

Adriana sat down and gathered herself.

"His name is Austin Agoria. He rides with a club called the One-Eyed Jacks. They run heroin all across the Midwest using people you would never expect to carry drugs—housewives, people in financial trouble, college kids, but mostly the unemployed. Anybody they can manipulate is a potential candidate.

"If you're desperate and need money, you're a potential runner for their operation. They like to use inconspicuous people. The more average-looking you are, the better. Conventional-looking, all-American citizens who draw no attention to themselves are far more likely to fly under the radar.

"Here's the way it goes. Each night before a delivery, you're instructed to leave one of your car doors unlocked—preferably the driver's side. The next day, your telephone rings, and a person pretending to be an old friend suggests a restaurant to meet for lunch.

"When you walk to your car to drive to your lunch date, you realize that someone was in your car the night before because the door you left unlocked is now locked. You drive to the restaurant, go inside, sit down, and have a meal. When you finish eating, you return to your car. An envelope with twelve hundred to fifteen hundred dollars is on the floorboard under the seat, just waiting for you. That's it.

"You never park your car where you can see it. So you don't see the person who puts the package in your car in the evening or the one who gets it out of your car while you're at the restaurant. You never know what you're transporting, and you can't identify anyone connected to the phone call.

"Most of the carriers just starting out thought this was a dream opportunity of a lifetime. That's how they suck you in. Your transports in the beginning are simple, easy, and low-key, but they don't stay that way. And there's a whole network of people involved in this operation, so you never know who is watching.

"After a while, they increase the traveling distances. Before you know it, you're traveling across state lines. One-day trips become three-day turnarounds. You never actually make contact with any-body; it's all completely anonymous. But if you get busted, it's all on you. You're a lone-wolf carrier with no apparent ties to anyone. There's no other way to play it since there's no one you can identify. Austin calls the carriers his 'sacrificial lambs.' "

Adriana unloaded another story about Austin's extortion practices.

"One time Austin withheld one of his runner's payoffs. He said he did it because he didn't like the way the guy looked at me. When the runner complained about not being paid, Austin turned around and accused him of stealing the package he was transporting. Austin told him if he didn't come up with ten thousand dollars, his wife would be raising his children on her own.

"When the runner came up with the money, Austin held a gun to his head and said, 'That money just bought you your life. One day, you can tell your children how close you came to the angel of death and how lucky you were to walk away. Now go home to your family, say your prayers, and be grateful that I let you live another day. And never forget you owe your life to me.' "

I sat and listened while Adriana filled me in on her psycho ex-boyfriend and the One-Eyed Jacks' drug trade. I said nothing about my previous encounter with them. I was beyond freaked out as my mind raced through all the hazardous possibilities. They knew where we lived. Our studio was off the street and out of the public eye. They could come right to our door at any time, day or night. No one would see them come or go. The police couldn't protect us. The letter we received wasn't an overt threat.

I sat silently digesting all the new information I had taken in. There was one more important thing I needed to know.

"Adriana, tell me what Austin looks like."

Adriana collected herself.

"He's about five ten, with blond hair. He slicks it back like they did in the fifties. I think they used to call it a jelly roll. He has bad skin. It gives him a ruddy appearance, and he has a cocky swagger to his walk. He carries himself like an athlete except he's not. He chain smokes Lucky Strikes when he's not smoking pot, and he's built like a wrestler. His hands and forearms are naturally muscular, and he has a dragon tattoo on the inside of his right forearm. I think he got the tattoo overseas when he was in the Navy. Believe it or not, that's where he made most of his drug connections."

My head was now reeling from the possibility that I knew this guy. Adriana just gave me the perfect description of one of the two thugs who robbed me and left me for dead in a dumpster. I needed to be absolutely sure.

"Adriana, does the dragon tattoo look oriental?"

"Yea. It's an oriental dragon tattoo. How did you know?"

"You're not the only one who's psychic."

Adriana was really frightened. She got real quiet and started pacing back and forth.

I was worried as well. It was all so unbelievable that I couldn't wrap my head around it. I couldn't fathom the possibility that Austin and the blonde-haired, crowbar-carrying cowboy who beat me half to death and left me to die were one and the same. *How fucking unbelievable is this?*

Adriana didn't know it, but through her, our lives would once again intersect. The coincidence of it blew me away.

I realized then and there that sitting in the studio, waiting for something to happen, was the worst possible option. It was time to vanish.

"Grab a couple of trash bags and gather your things. We're getting out of here tonight after it gets dark."

Adriana didn't argue. She filled two plastic trash bags with her belongings and started to fill one for me.

"Don't fill that one. I'm not going with you."

"What do you mean?" Adriana looked startled. I think she thought I was abandoning her.

I explained. "Austin probably knows who I am. He's come right to our front door. We were unbelievably lucky that neither of us was home when he paid us a visit. If we stay together, he'll wait for the perfect opportunity to close in and pounce. He's letting you know that he can get to you whenever he wants. He wants to get in your head before making his move.

"We have to stay one step ahead. We don't have enough money to leave town, but I know a place where you can go and disappear. It's not far away, but it's out of the way—if you know what I mean."

Adriana listened while I continued. "There's a small, run-down motel that rents little one-room bungalows by the week. It's old and it's seen better days, but it's cheap and it's a good place to hide until we come up with more money or a better plan."

We waited until dark, gathered the two trash bags, and walked down the stairs to leave. If anybody was watching, it looked like we were taking out our trash. Once we made our way downstairs,

Adriana set the trash bags next to the trash cans in the alley and waited for me to pick her up. I cut through the gangway to the car and drove around the block to make sure no one was following.

Once I was sure it was safe, I pulled into the alley to pick up Adriana. My heart stopped as I pulled up to the back-alley entrance to the studio. The two trash bags were stacked neatly next to the trash cans—right where I left them—but Adriana was gone.

I got out of the car and looked up and down the alley. A feeling of nausea started to overcome me as I considered the possibility that Austin abducted Adriana. *I never should have left her alone in the alley!*

My eyes darted everywhere in a panic, as I scanned my surroundings. A flicker of movement caught my attention. I looked up to the iron balcony at the back door entrance of my studio. Adriana was walking down the staircase. She saw me standing by the car and read the look on my face.

"I had to go to the bathroom!" she exclaimed.

"You scared me half to death!" I shouted. "Get in the car! Let's get outta here!"

I grabbed the trash bags, threw them in the car, and drove quickly out of the neighborhood, traveling the side streets. Eventually, I turned west on Highway 66.

⸻

After about twenty minutes, I knew we were getting close to the motel. I remembered it was easy to miss, so I slowed down and then stopped short at a small sign that read, Vacancy Casa Roma Motel. The light inside the sign was burned out, and the plastic veneer cover was so faded from sun exposure and weather that the words were hard to read.

I pulled down the driveway through the entrance and into a small asphalt courtyard. The courtyard was enclosed by dingy little bungalows, each one with a metal-roof carport next to the entrance-way. You could pull your car under the carport, take two steps, and get right into the entrance of your own private unit without being seen. The people who lived here were short-term transients who were so knee-deep in their own problems that they wouldn't bother themselves with a busy-body mentality. This place was perfect.

I told Adriana to wait in the car, while I went in to talk to the motel manager. His office was in the middle unit. As I walked through the doorway, I was immediately struck by the smell of cat urine. An extremely overweight old man looked up from the portable television he was watching and said, "Can I help you?" He seemed slightly aggravated.

His clothes were dirty, and the office was filled with old magazines, newspapers, and an overflowing trash can. He stared at me like I was intruding on the game show he was watching.

"How much for a room?"

"That depends on how long you want to stay. You can rent a room for four hours, six hours, eight hours, by the day, by the week, or by the month. It's all up to you."

"How much is it to rent a bungalow for the week?"

"That would be one hundred and twenty-five dollars," the old man said.

I paid in cash and started filling out the paperwork using a fake name and address. The old man didn't bother to check either one. *So far, this is far too easy.*

The old man didn't ask questions and he didn't bother to ask for an ID. He handed me two keys for bungalow number five and turned toward the TV. He wanted to get back to his game show.

"If you stay any longer, the next deposit is due a week from today, by six p.m." the old man said as I started for the door.

"I doubt if I'll be staying any longer than the week."

"That's what they all say, son," the old man said as he settled back into his *Wheel of Fortune.* "That's what they all say."

CHAPTER 17

I got back to the car and drove under the carport to bungalow number five, stopping next to the bungalow doorway. We got out of the car with Adriana's things and made our way in.

The room was tiny. It had a single wire-spring bed that took up most of the space in the room. The bathroom had a toilet and sink but no bathtub or shower. There was an air conditioner in the only window of the bungalow and a space heater that stuck out into a narrow aisle way that looked like it had seen better days. A beat-up dresser with a cracked mirror had cluttered remnants left behind by previous occupants. An old picture-tube television with rabbit ears sat in the corner. Adriana didn't complain.

This place was a shit-hole. I was aggravated. The room was so small, there was barely enough space to walk around the bed to the dresser. I didn't want to bitch about it. We checked in under the radar, and I wanted it to stay that way.

"I know this place is a hole," I said. "But I think you'll be safe here."

Adriana sat on the bed. She was trying not to show it, but I could tell she was really upset.

"I don't know if I can do this." Adriana said.

"I already paid a week in advance. I'm sorry about the room. But for now, I don't know that we have any other choice."

Adriana opened one of the trash bags, expecting to see her belongings. It was filled with loose trash, spoiled food scraps, and rancid-smelling baby diapers. In our hurried departure, I grabbed one of the wrong trash bags. It felt like it was exactly what we were handed—one great big, overwhelming pile of shit!

I sat down next to Adriana, took her hand, and folded her fingers between mine. "I don't know where all this is going, but I promise I'll never let anything happen to you. We're gonna get through this." It was a speech I wasn't too sure about.

"I'll go back to the studio later and pick up your things," I handed Adriana one of the two keys. "While we're here, try to keep a low profile. Don't go outside and don't let anybody in." She nodded her head in agreement.

"Try to get some rest," I said. I was hoping to get her to relax, but it was wishful thinking. We were both really keyed up.

More than anything, I wanted to make Adriana feel safe. But I didn't know if that was possible. I didn't feel safe myself, and Adriana knew it. There was no point in trying to project a false sense of confidence. Adriana knew me all too well. At this point, I was anything but confident.

What's next? I had no answers and no solutions. I was thinking like a victim. Every move we made up to this point was a reaction. It was like we were in this strange, peculiar no man's land. We weren't even sure where we were standing—shaky ground to be sure. It was unfamiliar and dangerous territory. *What to do?*

"I'll stay with you until you fall asleep. Then I have to go back to the studio."

Adriana changed into her nightgown and got in bed. I undressed and climbed in next to her. Neither of us could sleep. Adriana tossed and turned. My mind was racing, absorbed in the details of every-thing that unfolded in the last twenty-four hours. Time was drag-ging as we laid in silence.

I looked around the room at the stark, dreary condition of everything. There wasn't one thing in this shit-hole that wasn't totally worn out. Staying here was making me feel the same way.

I continued to examine the room. Unidentifiable stains tainted the drab-green color on the walls. It was probably nicotine. I hoped it was nicotine. I looked up at the only picture on the wall—dogs playing poker. They looked like they were having more fun than me. An ancient spider's web swung lazily from the ceiling over the bed. It held the hollow shell of a long-deceased insect carcass, hanging desperately at the end of a fragile thread—remnants of the last vic-tim that had probably been killed and devoured ages ago. Now we were hanging in the same place.

In a matter of a few hours, we went from a great life to a life of fear, turmoil, and uncertainty. Austin and the One-Eyed Jacks really had us scrambling.

I felt Adriana's hand wrap around my shoulder. "Roman, are you asleep?"

"No. I can't sleep either."

Adriana knew I was upset. "Why don't we take advantage of this sleazy motel? It might be good for both of us."

Adriana was trying to put me at ease. I turned around, and she had already slipped off her nightgown.

Adriana made it easy to forget about the predicament we were in—at least for the moment. She knew how to take my mind far away from the ugliness of what we were facing.

What we had ran deeper than mere physicality. When we were together, she gave me everything—100 percent of herself. She had the ability to wash away the influence of the rest of the world. I wanted to be able do the same for her. She knew I would try to protect her from any kind of threat—or at least die trying.

I realized that nothing else mattered. Adriana was the most important thing in my life, and no one was going to take that away. We never spoke about love, but that's what it was. Being this close was a gift. It brought a peaceful presence back to both of us. At that moment, I felt like everything was going to be OK—even though it wasn't.

I wanted so much to fall asleep and forget the nightmare of the day. But there was too much to deal with. I forced myself to get up and get dressed. I didn't want to leave, but I felt like I had no other choice.

I wanted this thing with Blondie to be over and done with. I wanted to get past all this and go back to living our lives. Right then and there, I realized the only way to get past the shit was to step in it. Sometimes you have to take out the trash. Things were going to get nasty—no doubt about it.

As I made my way to the door, I picked up the bag of trash and looked over at Adriana. She had fallen asleep. I wanted to kiss her goodbye, but I didn't want to wake her.

It was time to slip away and initiate my plan. I now knew exactly what I wanted to do and how I wanted to do it. It was time to settle an old score. It was time for retaliation, time to "do unto them what was done unto me."

I backed my car out of the carport, made a U-turn in the small asphalt courtyard, threw the trash bag in the dumpster, and drove out of the complex. As I headed toward the studio, I wondered how all this would turn out and how it would affect Adriana and me. I thought about her former life with Blondie. *Were his feelings for her as strong as mine?* This could prove to be quite a showdown.

My mind stayed focused on Blondie and all the possibilities where things could go wrong. There were too many to count. I had to admit it. Blondie got into my head. Now it was time for me to get into his.

I wanted to turn the tables on Blondie. I wanted to give him something to think about, but I didn't know if it was possible. I now had a plan, but a high degree of risk came with it. There are situations where planning goes only so far. This was one of those situations.

Austin and the One-Eyed Jacks were a major force to contend with. To be a One-Eyed Jack meant that you always had one eye on your brother. It was the creed they lived by—a kind of brotherhood. I was about to pick a fight with the whole family. It was a family of psychopaths that prided themselves in being an odd card in the deck—uniquely different, as in uniquely fucked up. To be a One-Eyed Jack meant you weren't the top card in the deck to begin with, so you had nothin' to lose. It was all about taking things to extremes, with no regard for the consequences.

At this point, I was ready to test their philosophy. I convinced myself it didn't matter anymore. I wanted Blondie and the One-Eyed Jacks to pay for what they did to me and Adriana. Still, I knew I would probably need help. I thought about locating Rubin and Stretch. *Would either one get involved in something as crazy as this after all these years?*

One thing was certain. Crazy was *exactly* what I needed.

I was desperate. No one in their right mind would be a part of what I was about to do. Rubin and Stretch were without question my only two options. Maybe I could convince them that all I needed was backup. Keep the One-Eyed Jacks off my back long enough for me to get to Blondie. That would be my pitch to Rubin and Stretch.

A quiet calm had taken over. I no longer cared about getting caught. I no longer cared about getting hurt. All I cared about was getting even. But how was I going to get to Blondie? That was my only question.

I had only one thing on my side—the element of surprise. The last thing Blondie expected was that I would come after him. I would seek him out in his own backyard. It would be the last place he would expect a confrontation.

One way or another, Blondie and the One-Eyed Jacks were gonna pay. I intended to keep my promise: They would never again be a threat to Adriana. As for me, the scars I carried ran deeper than my face. I wanted revenge.

When it got right down to it, I wanted more than revenge. I wanted to shake them to their core. I wanted to be the most destructive force they ever encountered. . . . I wanted to be their worst nightmare. . . .

It was time to go back to the studio, but I couldn't take the chance of parking close by. If Blondie was aware of me, my car would would let him know I was home. I parked the car on the next street over and walked between the gangway on the opposite side of the street. Then I crossed the alley and looked around to make sure nobody was watching. The alley was quiet and deserted. I grabbed Adriana's trash bag, and climbed the iron staircase.

Once inside, I went to my closet and found my aluminum mini-bat. It felt odd picking it up again after all these years. I thought about what it would feel like to be in a position where I actually *had* to bash somebody with it. . . . *When it got right down to it, would I be able to go through with it?* I was moving into uncharted territory.

I thought about Blondie and this incredible set of circumstances. I quickly dismissed the thought. There was much to do, and I had no time to waste on vengeful fantasies. The time for vengeance would come in real time. Fantasy Land was no longer an option.

I walked back to the entranceway door. It was the only way in or out of my studio. I locked both deadbolts and laid down on the bed. The last thing I wanted was to be caught sleeping, but I fell asleep almost as soon as my head hit the pillow. Getting caught in my studio would put me in a position of extreme vulnerability, but I needed the rest. The emotional events of the day had taken their toll. I was exhausted at every level. Sleep was a welcome relief.

When I woke up, I was instantly aware of the situation at hand. Adriana was in a safe place, and now that I was free from worrying about her, I was able to focus on what had to be done.

I was growing more and more tired of living a life of constantly having to look over my shoulder. If Austin and the One-Eyed Jacks were the ones who robbed me and left me to die, it was time to make them pay—not just for me but for Adriana as well. An inner rage was starting to grow.

I left the studio with only two items: my mini-bat and a ski mask.

CHAPTER 18

At this point I'd like to say that I'm a peace-loving person by nature. However, if threatened, everyone has the potential to cross into areas of the unknown. This is right where I was headed. I was about to start a war. The One-Eyed Jacks were about to encounter a *wild card* unlike anyone they previously encountered.

Up until now this was a silent, undeclared war—a war of thoughts with no action. All that was about to change. All I had was myself to depend on. I truly didn't care. It was almost like I derived some crazy sense of freedom from knowing that the only person they could get to was me. Adriana was in a safe place, and the Jacks had no idea that a serious threat was approaching. I don't know why, but I felt strangely protected by that thought. I remembered the old man's words: You choose the time and place. Choosing the time and place was now my highest priority.

As I remember . . .

There was this little sleaze ball cocktail lounge right next to a barbecue place. It was one of the two One-Eyed Jacks' hangouts that I knew of. As I drove by, I saw five motorcycles parked out front. I parked half a block away, around the corner on a quiet, deserted side street. I raised the hood of my jacket, slid the bat up my sleeve, put on my sunglasses, and stuffed the ski mask in my back pocket. Then I got out of my car and walked back to the bar.

The place was called Popeye's Pink Pussycat Lounge. Five of the Jacks were sitting at the bar. They were easy to identify. They were all wearing their colors intently watching the show.

The crowd was light, the music was loud, and the dancers were so high they were almost falling off the stage from whatever form of intoxication they were into. The dancers were dressed in pussy-cat whiskers and pink-fur bikinis. They were in rare form. No one paid any attention to my entrance.

The One-Eyed Jacks were enjoying themselves. They reminded me of vultures waiting for an opportunity to take advantage of fallen prey. They were waiting for floundering pink pussies to fall into their lap. I was there to take advantage of a similar opportunity. While they were waiting for floundering pink pussies, I was waiting for a wild-card opportunity. It was time to see who was gonna fuck who.

I sat in a booth at the back of the bar and waited. A fat, bullet-breasted waitress with skin-tight spandex pants and heavy fake eyelashes asked me what I was having. I ordered a Crown on the rocks and reached for my wallet when she came back with my drink. It was time to pay the waitress. It caught me off guard.

I was relieved no one noticed as I struggled to retrieve my wallet from my back pocket with the wrong hand. The closest hand to my wallet was holding the bat up my sleeve. The waitress was completely disinterested. She walked to another table after I paid her. I sat back in the booth and waited.

The show was pathetic—no talent, sloppy drunk exhibitionism, no doubt about it—but I watched it anyway. Vulgar was one step above what I was witnessing. There was nothing sexy about it, but there was a lot goin' on. I watched the crowd as well. This was like a freak show. The crowd was really into it. Drunkin' hard-ons, the whole lot of 'em, hypnotized by the outrageous display. I couldn't tell who was more distasteful—the performers or the crowd.

The Jacks were hypnotized as well, mesmerized into an alcoholic fantasy land. It was a good sign. The closer they were to unconscious, the better. I was there to take 'em the rest of the way.

I settled back, taking in the moment, watching, waiting, and drinking. What an incredible bunch of fuck-ups!

It was like watching an X-rated version of *The Gong Show*. Too bad I had other plans. Distraction wasn't part of my agenda. I was getting motivated. The grand finale was waiting with a bat up his sleeve.

If only Blondie was here, I could end this thing right now and get it over with. Maybe I'll get lucky, and he'll come strollin' in like a peacock. Wouldn't that just be the shit!

I leaned forward and continued to sip my drink. My other arm hung straight by my side, my hand curled around the butt end of the bat. I had an odd thought: *The crowd has a rocket in their pocket, and I have a jackhammer up my sleeve.*

What a crazy situation this was! Things couldn't get much more bizarre. I kept telling myself to try to stay cool.

I guess it was about four or five songs before the opportunity presented itself. I noticed the song playing in the background. It was a Boz Scaggs tune—called Lowdown. It was a sign from the universe as far as I was concerned.

I was thinking about the irony of the title and what I was about to do when two of the Jacks got up to go to the men's room. That left three at the bar. I took my sunglasses off with my free hand and slid them casually into my jacket pocket. I waited another thirty seconds before making my way into the men's room.

I found the first One-Eyed Jack standing at the urinal. The other one was in a locked stall. It was just the three of us. I locked the door from the inside. A steady calm took over as I let the bat slide out of my sleeve and grasped the smooth, thin handle.

I took the Jack standing at the urinal out with one shot. With a muffled thud and a grunt, he fell to the floor. He laid there silent and unconscious, in an ever-expanding puddle of his own urine.

His partner in the stall heard him fall and called out to him, but there was no answer. I went over to the light switch and turned out the light. The Jack in the stall called out to his friend once again, but to no avail. He started to curse. He thought his friend was playing a practical joke. As he continued calling out to his friend, his voice grew cautious. Somehow, he sensed he was in danger.

I heard him flush the toilet and unlatch the stall door. My eyes were starting to adjust to the darkness. I waited at the side of the stall for the door to open. That's when I caught sight of his pistol. I swung the bat around and slammed it on the top of his wrist and thumb. The blow launched his pistol to the floor.

We were now face-to-face in the dark. All I could see was the outline of his silhouette. I shoved the butt end of the bat into the shadow of his face, knocking him back against the wall. He tried to swing at me, but he moved in slow motion. He must have been really drunk. *Too bad for him.*

My next shot took him to the floor. I followed up with an extra kick to the head to make sure he wouldn't get up. He just laid there. I turned the lights back on and recovered his pistol from the floor.

I was lucky the gun didn't go off when I smashed his thumb and wrist. It would have taken the surprise away from what I was about to do.

After untucking my shirt, I stuck the automatic inside the front of my pants, leaving my shirt out to conceal it. Next I put on my ski mask but before I did, I looked at both Jacks to see if they were still breathing. They both were still alive. One was twitching and flailing, not a good sign.

I knew at this point that I crossed some kind of line, but I didn't care. I wanted to make them all pay. If they were in a coma, so be it. I knew firsthand what that was all about. It was now up to me to wrap this up with the remaining three and get out without being identified.

The noise outside the men's room was rowdy and unrelenting. The pink pussycats still had the crowd engaged in the frolicking unconscious escapades of tasteless tavern entertainment. It was time to exit the men's room and rock the house. With a ski mask over my face and bat in hand, I exited the men's room and headed for the three Jacks at the bar.

My quick advance came as a complete surprise. The first Jack at the bar never saw it comin'. I took him out with one shot to the head. After the loud crack of the bat, there was a moment of dead silence as the freak show came to an abrupt halt. The crowd was trying to process what was going on. They were all shocked into a strange kind of stupor.

The other two Jacks were as unprepared as the crowd. I moved on to One-Eyed Jack number two. He had the presence of mind to reach for a gun. I slammed the bat sideways into the side of his arm. The blow landed with a crack to his elbow, and the pistol flew from his hand and landed under a table.

As he made a move to retrieve his gun, I bashed his leg with a side swing to the knee and followed up with a shot to the head. He fell to the floor immediately. He was clutching his knee and screaming his ass off. I bashed him one more time with a head shot. He instantly quieted down. I remembered the pain of that very same kind of blow, but I felt no compassion or remorse. I had a job to do.

The crowd was now in a frightened state of panic. But I was oblivious to their cries. There was one more One-Eyed Jack to deal with. I went after him like a shark after a mackerel, but he dove head first over the bar. It was a smart move on his part, but it didn't save him. As he slowly raised his head up from the back of the bar, I bashed the top of his skull. It was like playing whack-a-mole with a baseball bat. He didn't get up.

One dumb-ass customer started to go for the gun on the floor.

"Go for that gun, and I'll knock your fucking head off," I said as I moved closer. He knew I was serious and stayed right where he was.

I looked over at the bartender. He was wielding a wooden baseball bat of his own. He must have had it tucked away behind the bar. We both stood there facing each other—each of us positioned to fight from our own respective sides of the bar. Both of us had bats in hand, but the bartender wasn't prepared to use his. I could see in his face that his stance was nothing more than a defensive posture. He wanted no part of this type of confrontation. That was fine with me. It was a momentary standoff.

The pink pussycats screamed and shrieked as the horrified patrons stared in shock and disbelief. I was a masked marauder with a violent destructive agenda—a crazed raging wrecking machine with unknown intentions. This wasn't a robbery. It was a flat-out insane assault.

A large glass pitcher of beer stood alone on a nearby table top, abandoned by patrons in their attempt to flee from danger. I wound up, and bashed the pitcher with everything I had. Shattered bits of broken glass and beer splattered and sprayed the crowd in a volatile release of explosive force. I was sending a message to the crowd: Don't cross my path! Don't challenge me! The crowd watched paralyzed—scared into a state of dumbfounded silence.

A grave stillness once again descended upon the room. We all stared at each other for a moment before I took the opportunity to leave.

Nobody tried to challenge me on the way out. Once outside, I dropped my hood, pulled off the ski mask, and ran around the corner to my car. Driving off undetected was what I was hoping for.

<hr />

My heart was pounding like a jackhammer as I drove away. It was an incredible feeling. I had just become a living metaphor of my imagination.

I stopped the car about four or five blocks away and parked on a side street. I was looking for a place to pitch the gun. I got out of my car and pitched the pistol in a sewer, making sure nobody was watching. What I had just done was more than enough to put me in jail for a long time. Being caught with a gun would only make matters worse. I wasn't sure if anybody saw me run away from the bar. If they saw me get in the car and got my license number I was sure to be arrested. I went back to my car and drove home to my studio.

Once inside, I closed the door and sat down. This was without question the wildest, craziest, and by far the stupidest thing I had ever done. What's more, it accomplished almost nothing. Blondie wasn't even there!

What if someone saw me running down the street and took my license number? I'd end up in jail, and Adriana would have to deal with this mess on her own. I tried to push these thoughts out of my head, but the thoughts persisted. Another thought occurred to me. How was I any different from Blondie?

Here I was wrapped up in the same kind of insanity that Adriana was running from to begin with. *What would she think of all this?*

I ignored all the warnings—dismissed them as quickly as they came to me. It was better that Adriana didn't know.

I have to keep all of this separate from her. It was the wrong path to follow.

My energy was still through the roof. I was still running full out, on all cylinders, and the pedal was stuck to the floor. I paced around the studio, trying to unwind. It was like I was charged with some secret source of super-high-voltage energy. I was adrenalin man! No one could stop me like this!

It took about an hour before I realized that I actually got away with it—in broad daylight none-the-less. I also have to acknowledge that as crazy and stupid as this stunt was, part of me was proud that I actually got away with it. I have to admit it. I got off on it.

From now on, I'll have to plan things with a lot more precision and forethought. It's one thing to take risks and another thing altogether to be stupid.

This encounter also made me realize what an uphill battle I was facing. It was at this point that I truly felt like it was me against the world.

I needed to come back to reality. I needed to look in the mirror and see with clear eyes who was staring back. I knew I wasn't big, and I knew I wasn't bad. I had better be smart.

Who was I kidding? Nothing about any of this was smart, but I was blind to all of it. I was swimming in glorious victory, wrapped up in my own private war—poisonous water to be sure. Victory can be a seductive, intoxicating whore. Once you get a taste, you can chase it straight to hell.

I was farther down the rabbit hole than I realized. But my only thought at the time was to keep going.

I had two advantages: No one knew who I was, and no one knew what my motives and intentions were. I was a nameless, faceless mystery. An ominous, unknown enemy is far more threatening and intimidating than one who's been identified. Not knowing who or what is coming after you is a fearsome thing to have to deal with.

This singular thought gave me the motivation to continue. I was confident that Blondie and the One-Eyed Jacks had more than their fair share of enemies. I hoped this fact would keep me anonymous—at least for a little while.

The war was just beginning. Again, I thought of the old man's rules. The One-Eyed Jacks got caught with their pants down. It was the kind of bare-assed down-for-the-count, kick-in-the-nuts first shot that made your asshole pucker just thinkin' about it.

How will the One-Eyed Jacks react? What are they thinking? Over and over, these questions invaded my consciousness. I finally dismissed them. It really didn't matter. A new plan had come to mind. Everything was starting to come together. The old man's philosophy was proving itself to be right as rain.

And through it all, I learned something of great value: One or two good shots can change everything, even if the odds are stacked against you.

Keep moving forward, and keep the Jacks off balance—this was my new direction.

The situation was escalating, and I had the momentum. I had at least one more stunt up my sleeve besides the mini-bat. I was about to get creative in a destructive sort of way.

It was time to put one of the few skills I had to good use, time to send a personal message to Blondie, time to unleash one of the most destructive forces of my trade. It was time to poke the serpent.

CHAPTER 19

It was now late in the afternoon, and I needed to get back to the old neighborhood. I made my way out of my studio being careful not to be seen. After a cautious and wary approach, I got to my car unnoticed, put the mini-bat under the seat, and headed to the old neighborhood with my weapon of choice. But on the way, I had to make a pit stop.

Welder's Steel and Industrial Supply was a business I was very familiar with. I purchased glasses, leather gloves, spark igniters, and leather coveralls from them many times in the past. I had a charge account with them, and my credit was good. Today, I would be purchasing something a little more expensive.

I went in and bought a portable cutting torch complete with hoses, pressure regulators, mini-acetylene and oxygen tanks, and cutting goggles. I had the bottles filled and put the torch assembly kit together right in the showroom. I asked if I could test the torch, and the manager showed me to a workbench at the back of the store where he let me cut several pieces of scrap metal plate.

After adjusting the gauges to the proper settings, I tested my new equipment. The torch performed beautifully. It cut through the metal plate quickly and effortlessly—like a hot knife through butter, as they say in the trade.

My gauges were set, and my tanks were full. Now all I had to do was find Blondie's motorcycle and cut it to pieces. I had never dissected a motorcycle with a cutting torch before. Doing it without getting caught would be quite an undertaking. I was up for the challenge.

I left the supply house and set out for the only other One-Eyed Jacks' hangout that I knew of—the Swagger In. The Swagger In was a bar down off South Broadway, close to the river. Everybody knew it was a biker hangout and one of their home bases. If I was gonna find Blondie, it would probably be there.

I got there early in the evening. Seven motorcycles were parked out front. There was nothing left for me to do but wait to see if Blondie was inside. I waited until it got dark.

Sometimes revenge requires patience. I had never stalked anyone before. What an incredible waste of time! My only consolation was that I was no longer thinking like a victim. Still, time was dragging.

I was almost ready to give up when Blondie and six of the Jacks strolled out of the bar. I couldn't see Blondie up close, but I was almost positive it was him. He had a certain look and a cocky gate to his walk that set him apart. That slicked-back blonde hair was a dead giveaway.

The group rode together with me tailing behind at a distance. None of them noticed as I followed. They were all liquored up and not paying much attention. One by one they started to taper off— each going his own separate way.

I stayed with Blondie at a distance and followed until he turned into an alley. I couldn't follow him any closer without being noticed, so I circled around the block to enter the alley from the opposite end of the street. I drove slowly, hoping to catch a glimpse of his residence.

As I turned the corner, I noticed the alley was clear. No one was in sight. Blondie had probably already parked his motorcycle and was somewhere in this block. No way could he just disappear right out of thin air. He wasn't fuckin' Houdini.

I drove slowly down the alley, on the lookout for him or his motorcycle. The back of my neck tightened as I scanned the back-yards and residences on each side of the alley. I knew he was close.

Suddenly, I noticed an inside light turn off through the window of a small, single-unit garage. As I slowly passed by, I saw Blondie walk from the garage across the yard to his back door. He was fumbling his keys.

I now knew where Blondie lived. *His motorcycle must be parked in that garage.*

I drove past the rear of Blondie's residence, turned out of the alley, and parked my car on a side street around the corner.

Again I played the waiting game. I had to make sure Blondie was asleep. If he caught me doing what I was about to do, it would surely be the end of me.

I opened my glove compartment and removed a pen and a scrap piece of paper. It was time to write a note to Blondie.

The note had five words printed in big, bold letters. "I KNOW WHERE YOU LIVE." I folded the note in half and put it in my back pocket. Next, I grabbed the flashlight from the glove box, got out of the car, and removed my portable cutting torch and tanks from the trunk, along with a spark igniter, pliers, and an ice pick.

I started the long walk down the alley to Blondie's garage. My heart pounded with every step. It was a creepy walk down the alley. I felt completely isolated—like I was the last living person left on earth.

It's time to go to work.

When I got to the garage, I noticed the heavy-duty padlock and metal folding latch that secured the sliding-panel door. I was in luck. I could gain access to the garage from the alley-side entrance. All I had to do was cut the lock. Luckily, the garage blocked me from being seen from the house.

I looked up and down the alley. I wanted to make sure I wasn't being watched. The alley was eerily quiet. I lit the torch with the spark igniter, being careful not to pop the flame. When it ignited, I adjusted the flame and immediately directed the heat onto the padlock. I wanted to get out of the alley and into the garage as fast as possible.

The heat from the torch quickly turned the U-shaped curve of the lock a bright orange. I lightly pressed the oxygen handle on the torch. The smooth flow of air blew the heated metal away instantly. After slowly shutting down the gases to the torch, I removed the lock with a small pliers. There's no such thing as padlock security when you have a cutting torch in your hands.

So far, this is just too easy.

I flipped open the steel latch and slowly slid open the garage door. It didn't make a sound. As I made my way inside, I was cautious and methodical. I was in within seconds.

Entering Blondie's garage was like entering a dark, forbidden cavern.

Slowly and quietly, I closed the panel door behind me. The ominous silence fueled an added uncertainty and excitement. *This shit is like an adrenalin rush times ten.* The only thing I could hear was my shallow breathing and my heart pounding.

I turned on my flashlight, and there before my eyes was a sight to behold—a 1972 dark-maroon custom metal-flake V Twin Harley Shovel Head. The engine was still slightly warm.

What I'm about to do to this beautiful work of art is a damn shame.

Suddenly, I heard a door open. I turned my flashlight off and held my breath. It was the next-door neighbor. He had just let his dog out to do his business. Time stood still, and so did I.

If he leaves the dog out all night, what am I gonna do?

I stood motionless in the dark for around twenty minutes before he let his dog back in.

This unexpected setback unnerved me to the point that I seriously considered bailing out. But I hung in there. To be truthful, I was too scared to move.

After a few more agonizing minutes, I decided it was time to go to work. I turned my flashlight back on and allowed my eyesight to refocus. It felt good to breathe again.

I approached the bike and quietly laid it on the ground. Any unwanted noise at this point would surely give me away. I reignited the torch, slowly adjusted the flame, and started immediately to apply heat to the maroon metal-flake frame. An added glow from the torch cast a soft, incandescent radiance on the room. It was a nice atmosphere for a motorcycle about to experience death.

As I applied heat to the front frame, the paint instantly melted and the metal quickly started to glow. I carefully cut the front fork off the motorcycle. The front wheel and fork silently fell away. Then I cut the frame separating the back wheel from the rest of the bike. Next, I cut the drive chain and separated the back wheel from the frame as best I could. Finally, I cut the frame around the engine into multiple pieces, being careful not to cut into any gas lines.

I cut through all the spokes on both wheels. I didn't want any part of the bike to be salvageable. I even burned some of the chrome off the engine and wheel rims. I wanted to do as much damage as possible, but it was taking too long. I was already pushing my luck.

I cut brake lines and handlebars, melted the padding on the seat, and finished by lightly brushing the flame over the red metal-flake gas tank—just enough to burn and blacken that beautiful maroon-metallic paint. After I finished, I shut down the flame, again being careful not to pop the torch. The last thing I did was slash both tires and puncture the gas tank with the ice pick. My mission was almost complete.

The bike was laying before me in pieces. As I looked down at the smoldering heap of what used to be a motorcycle, a deep sense of satisfaction came over me.

A putrid odor of burnt leather and naugahyde mixed with the smell of burnt metallic paint and metal. The acidic smell burned my lungs. I instinctively took shallow breaths. I knew the air wasn't healthy. There was nothing about any of this that was healthy.

I could also smell the melted steel and burnt paint as it mixed with the stale humid air of the garage. A heavy smoke hung like fog in the air.

So this is what a dead motorcycle smells like.

I took the note from my back pocket and laid it face up on the gas tank. It was time to go.

I picked up my portable torch and quietly exited the garage, leaving the same way I came in. But before I shut the door, I took one more final look at that smoldering pile of shit that laid in pieces on the concrete floor. Then I turned off my flashlight, slowly slid the panel door closed, and walked away.

As I walked down the alley to my car, I thought I was home free when an angry German Shepherd suddenly barked and snarled at me from a fenced-in yard. His hair was up on his back, and he was glaring and growling with vicious intent like a demon from the underworld. He looked like a giant wolf on steroids. He was showing large, ominous teeth. Judging by their size, I'd say he was immensely proud of them. He was extremely agitated. He was letting me know who's boss. There would be no argument from me.

That dog scared the living shit out of me! I thought I was gonna have a heart attack! If I did die from a heart attack, I was pretty sure I could get him a job guarding the gates of hell.

I collected myself and walked on to my car. I was almost home free.

When I got to my car, I put all my tools in the trunk and drove away undetected to my studio. It was early in the morning, but it was still dark. My sense of time, along with my anxiety, was gone. I felt a deep sense of jubilation during the ride home.

What a day and night it's been.

I wished I could see Blondie's face when he discovered his motorcycle in pieces. I wished I could see his face when he read my note.

Exhaustion was starting to rear it's ugly head, but I had to keep going. There was still more to do. I couldn't afford to make any mistakes. I couldn't afford to leave anything undone.

Once I got home, I took the remaining money from the mattress—seven hundred and fifty dollars. I grabbed the mini-bat and dead-bolted both locks on the door. I wanted to lay down for just a second. This time, it wasn't my intention to fall asleep, but I fell asleep almost immediately. I didn't wake up until late the next morning.

When I eventually did wake up, I was alarmed upon awakening. I couldn't believe I slept for so long.

If Blondie found his motorcycle, he'd surely be here soon with a vengeance. He'll recognize his own threatening words from the note he left on our door. It won't be long until he comes calling.

I left the studio as fast as possible with money and bat in hand. I got down to the bottom of the steps when I remembered the plastic trash bag full of Adriana's things that I left behind the night before. I went back up the steps and into the studio to retrieve it. If I didn't bring it back, Adriana would have a grand-mal conniption fit.

When I got to my car, I questioned whether I should have left the note on Blondie's motorcycle. After all, being anonymous was a huge advantage. But at this point, I no longer cared about being identified. Fuck him.

I wanted Blondie to know who I was. I wanted the threat to be blatant. However, it was still possible that he didn't know who I was. All Blondie knew for sure was that someone else besides Adriana was involved. I still might be an unknown. This possibility gave me confidence. I felt like I had the momentum. I left my studio undetected—another lucky break.

On my way back, I thought about how foolish I was allowing myself to fall asleep in my studio. I never should have left myself in that kind of vulnerable position. It was unbelievably careless. If Blondie would have caught me sleeping, it would all be over. I was lucky to get away with it. Luck was a companion seldom present in my life, but after last night, I had no complaints.

I now knew exactly what I had to do. I had just jumped into this thing with both feet. Once you step in shit, it's hard to get the odor off—even after you scrape it off your shoe. The stink of this whole thing would stay with me until I saw it all the way through.

It was time to go back to the old neighborhood. It was time to find Rubin and Stretch.

CHAPTER 20

I was on my way to Grand Bowl. Everybody who worked there or hung out there knew Rubin and Stretch. Both Rubin and Stretch were banned from the bowling alley for life.

As the story goes, Rubin threw a cue ball at Sleeper, a veteran high-stakes pool player that most everybody had sense enough to stay away from—everybody except Rubin. The two had a money dispute over a game of nine ball. Rubin was losing his ass, and Sleeper started to heckle him over it.

"You shoot pool like old people fuck," was the insult that pushed Rubin over the edge. Rubin had his fill, picked up the cue ball, and launched a line drive at Sleeper's head. Sleeper side-stepped the throw, and an innocent bystander took the shot full-force in the face. It knocked the poor guy unconscious. The police were called, and Rubin was arrested for assault.

As the police escorted him away, Rubin was told by management never to return to the bowling alley or he would be arrested.

When Stretch found out what happened, he flew up to the bowling alley, climbed the stairs, and made his way to the pool tables. Stretch snatched a tray of billiard balls and started throwing line drives into the liquor stock. Neatly displayed liquor bottles, along with glass shelves and large, decorative mirrors, exploded in unison as the bartender and patrons stared in amazement. Stretch was on a rampage!

This kind of mayhem was far beyond the bartender's area of expertise. Besides, he was way too fat to climb over the bar and stop him. By the time he waddled his fat ass around the bar, the damage was done. The police were called once again. The bowling alley was closed for the day, and Stretch was later arrested for vandalism, destruction of property, creating a public nuisance, and peace disturbance. He was also banned for life from the bowling alley and told never to return.

Before he went to jail, Stretch was sent to a state-authorized hospital psychiatrist for a psychological evaluation and a fit-for-confinement clearance. When the doctor asked why he committed such a senseless act, Stretch confessed that he knew his friend Rubin was going to jail and he wanted to keep him company.

Stretch's jail time lasted a bit longer than Rubin's. When he finally got out, he was in much better physical condition. There was nothing to do inside but exercise, but that wouldn't matter. Stretch wasn't going anywhere.

Once I arrived at the bowling alley, I climbed the stairs and started asking where I could find Rubin and Stretch. That's when I learned that Stretch had been killed. I heard about it from Jimmy the Snitch. Jimmy the Snitch was the neighborhood gossip who knew everything about everybody. He was also a lifer who never left the neighborhood. People used to say, "If Jimmy the Snitch didn't know about it, it didn't happen."

Jimmy said that Stretch had been drinking a six pack right outside his favorite package liquor store—a place called Liquor Quicker. The owner called the police after repeated attempts to convince Stretch to vacate the front of the store. The police arrived and informed Stretch that he had to leave the premises or he would be arrested.

This routine was an all too common experience for Stretch. He was angry and frustrated. He wasn't bothering anybody. Why couldn't they just leave him alone?

Stretch walked away and started his long walk home. He put on his headphones, cranked up the volume, and resigned himself to one more failed attempt to win out over yet another public nuisance hassle.

Stretch decided to take a shortcut home and walk the railroad tracks. While he was walking the tracks, a train approached him from behind. The engineer blew the train whistle and applied his emergency brakes, but to no avail. The loud music blasting in his ears covered the sound of the approaching train. Poor Stretch didn't have a chance. He never saw it coming. He was killed instantly.

Jimmy the Snitch was a long-time friend to Stretch. They grew up together on the same block. Jimmy finished the story by saying, "Stretch went out with a beer in his hand, and that's just the way he would have wanted it." Spoken like a true numb-nuts from the neighborhood.

Stretch's death came as a complete shock. I asked about Rubin.

"Rubin was just released from city jail on drug charges," according to another patron of the bowling alley.

I asked if anybody knew where Rubin was living.

"He lives in an apartment over his ex-girlfriend's tavern on Cherokee Street," piped up another veteran of the neighborhood.

"Thanks," I said, and left the bowling alley in hot pursuit of Rubin.

Rubin's ex-girlfriend's tavern was only a few blocks away, at the corner of Cherokee and Compton—a real elegant and fashionable establishment called Gopher Beaver Lounge. I made my way up to his residence and knocked on the door. I was almost ready to leave when Rubin finally responded to my persistent knock.

"Who is it?" Rubin asked. He seemed aggravated by the disturbance.

"It's Roman."

"Who?"

"Bat Man," I finally said. "It's Bat Man."

Rubin opened the door immediately. He was really glad to see me. We talked for a long time. We talked about the old days. We talked about Stretch's accident. We talked about who married who, and who got pregnant, and who went to jail, and who got out.

Rubin said he just got out and needed some cash. He looked terrible. He had needle tracks on his arms, and he was real thin. His clothes smelled like he hadn't showered in a week.

I was shocked by his condition, but I didn't say anything. I opened my wallet and handed him forty dollars. He was grateful for the cash.

This was not the same Rubin I knew. His face had hardened and his presence seemed more threatening. The only thing that looked the same were those crazy eyes and that dead-eye stare.

Rubin's look often made the rank-and-file community uncomfortable. Almost everyone avoided direct eye contact. Sometimes he just plain creeped people out. I wondered to what degree his appearance sabotaged his life.

I remembered a time many years earlier when I told Rubin there was no doubt in my mind that he could stare down a rattlesnake if that was his intention. His only comment was, "I got my old man's eyes and my mother's cold heart." It was a strange thing to say. I never heard Rubin mention his parents again.

Rubin's comment made me curious. I eventually got around to asking Stretch if he knew anything about Rubin's parents. Stretch confided with some reservation that Rubin's mother and father were both raging alcoholics. Rubin's father killed his mother late one night in a drunken rage—right in front of Rubin. Rubin was only five years old at the time. Rubin's father went to prison, and Rubin went into an orphanage. Stretch said Rubin lived there for two years until his grandmother petitioned the court for custody. According to Stretch, Rubin's father committed suicide in prison by hanging himself.

Rubin's grandmother once confided to Stretch that when Rubin came out of the orphanage, he had changed. According to his grandmother, Rubin was "never the same again." I never understood exactly what she meant by that.

There was no way to bring clarity to any of it. Rubin's only known relative was his grandmother, and she had passed on years ago. No one would know the truth of it without asking Rubin, and no way was that ever going to happen—not as far as I was concerned. Rubin's actual history would forever remain a mystery.

Remembering this story made me contemplate Rubin's life. I wondered if he was truly courageous or if he had a death wish.

All these thoughts were making my head swim. *Did I make a mistake in coming here? Should I drag him into this? What to do?*

After seeing Rubin in this condition, I wondered if I should back off and deal with this mess on my own. After all, it was my problem, and I had already taken steps to make it escalate. How would Rubin react to all this? The only thing I knew for sure about Rubin was that he was totally unpredictable. What to do?

Rubin thanked me again for the money. I think he was a little suspicious. After all, I hadn't seen him in years, and now I show up at his doorstep and just hand him forty dollars. He finally got around to asking why I had come to see him.

I told Rubin the whole story. I told him about my getting robbed, beaten, and left for dead. I told him about my blond-haired attacker and the dragon tattoo on his right inside forearm. I told him about Adriana and how she was on the run from a guy with the same blonde hair and the same dragon tattoo on his arm. I told him I believed this guy shaking down Adriana was the same guy who robbed me and left me to die in a dumpster. I told him this was more than just a coincidence.

I told him I believed it was fate that brought us all together and that it was up to me to put an end to it one way or another. I said I wanted revenge for what he did to me and what he was still doing to Adriana. I told him about the anonymous note left at my studio and how Adriana was afraid to go home.

I told him about Blondie's biker ties and his drug operation. I told him about my "batting practice" at Popeye's Pussy Cat Lounge. I told him about my torch-cutting chopper dissection in Blondie's garage the night before and the message I left on Blondie's gas tank.

I told him I was into this thing way too deep to do anything less than see it all the way through. In short, I told Rubin everything.

Rubin sat in silence for a long time. I was waiting for him to say, "Go fuck yourself." That was what he should say. If he did, I wouldn't blame him.

Rubin finally looked up and asked, "When are we going after this motherfucker?"

I couldn't believe it. Rubin still felt a kind of loyalty to me. I didn't even have to ask. He knew why I had come.

"Rubin," I said, "you're a lot better friend to me than I've been to you."

It was true. When I was younger, I went out of my way to stay away from Rubin. Now, after all these years, Rubin was still there for me. I felt like a total hypocrite. I didn't show it, but I was embarrassed and ashamed. It took a moment for me to get it together.

"Rubin," I finally said, "I don't want you in the middle of this. All I want from you is backup. If you can, I want you to keep Blondie's biker club off my back long enough for me to get to him. Distract them anyway you can if it comes down to it. Throw a chair, a beer bottle, turn the tables over—anything you can do to keep it between just him and me. I just want a shot at this prick.

"If things get really ugly, save yourself and get the fuck outta there. I can live with the consequences. All I'm lookin' for is a chance to take him down in his home territory, where he's the most comfortable—right in front of his biker buddies. I want to send Blondie and his biker clan a message they'll never forget.

"I'll pick you up tomorrow afternoon around two o'clock if you're up for it. We can figure out the rest when we get there. Are you OK with that?"

"I'll see you tomorrow at two," Rubin answered, "don't be late."

"Oh, and Rubin," I said as I walked out the door, "if you change your mind, I'll understand."

Rubin was smiling. "You just make sure you show up. If you don't, I'll have to come after you and kick the shit out of you. You know I'll do it, too."

"Just like the old days." I said, "Looks like it's down to Bat Man and Rubin." We both busted a gut laughing!

"Get the fuck outta here," Rubin said. "I'll see you tomorrow."

CHAPTER 21

I went back to Casa Roma. Adriana was angry with me—and obviously still upset. I understood why. I left her in the dark in this hole of a motel with no food, no transportation, and no explanation.

"Where have you been?"

"I'm sorry. I had to hook up with an old friend. It's been a long time since we've seen each other, and we had a lot catching up to do. He's gonna help us straighten this thing out."

"What are you about to do?"

"I'm gonna get the monkey off our back once and for all. I'm really tired of having to look over my shoulder. This bullshit has got to stop."

Adriana continued to question me.

"Who is this old friend, and what are you two up to?"

"He's an old friend from the neighborhood. I've known him since we were teenagers. He's gonna help us, but I can't say any more about it right now."

Adriana was pissed. "Ya know what's bullshit? You coming home after two days and not letting me in on what's going on. You were gone for two days Roman! Is that all you got to say?"

I didn't answer. Revealing my plans, would only give her more to worry about. She was right. I was caught between a rock and a hard place. Adriana continued to press me.

"You need to be straight with me Roman. I'm tired of this!"

"I'm tired of it too. That's why I hooked up with my friend. He understands the position we're in, and he's one of the few people I trust."

Adriana wanted to fight. Our emotions were worn really thin. I knew at the heart of her anger was a heartfelt concern for me. More than anything I wanted to be straight with her, but I couldn't bring myself to tell her the truth. So I deflected. I felt bad about it, but I did it anyway.

"Look," I said, "I'm doing everything I can to resolve this mess. The last thing I need right now is a fight with you. You either trust me or you don't."

Adriana finally backed off. "There's thirty-five dollars in my purse. Take the money and go get us some food. I haven't eaten since you left."

I was glad to have a reason to leave. Food has a way of mending fences. I hoped that eating together would put us on better terms. I told myself I'd make it up to her later, and slipped out the door.

There was a diner about a half mile from Casa Roma. As I drove there, I grew more and more bitter about Blondie's intrusion on our life. We never fought before he came into the picture. Living like this was starting to take its toll. I wanted to make Blondie pay—now more than ever. Tomorrow couldn't come soon enough.

I returned to the bungalow with burgers, fries, and extra-large chocolate shakes. The fries were still hot and steamy, and the burgers were juicy and delicious. We ate in silence, enjoying the meal as best we could. I was distracted the rest of the evening. Adriana knew me well enough to leave it alone. That night, we slept together in silence, curled up together in this tiny, old wire-spring single bed. After our earlier confrontation, it felt good to be close. I drifted off. My mind filled with questions about what tomorrow would bring.

The next day, we both got up early and got dressed. I was itching to go. I asked Adriana if she wanted me to get her some breakfast before I left, but she said she wasn't hungry. I kissed her goodbye and told her not to worry. I left more money on the dresser and said I would be back by early evening.

I didn't have to pick up Rubin until two o'clock. There was plenty of time to scout out Blondie's hangout—the Swagger In. But first, I drove to my brother's house and gave him the rest of the money. I gave him all I had, and kept back a hundred. I knew I might need a little money to carry out my plan. If things went totally wrong, I didn't want to get caught with a lot of cash. If I ended up taking another beat down—or worse—I wanted Blondie to get as little as possible.

When I got to my brother's place, he asked me what was goin' on. I ignored the question and offered no explanation. I asked if I could count on him to give Adriana the money. He assured me he would handle it, but he looked disgusted.

It was just like Rocky to be disgusted with me. He didn't approve of my friends, and he didn't approve of me. He knew I was up to something, and he didn't like it. Like Adriana, he knew I was being deceptive.

I couldn't help it. I knew Rocky would never get involved in anything like this. I didn't expect him to. He wasn't anything like me.

He was my older brother, but I never expected him to look out for me. I always looked out for myself. I didn't want him to worry, and I didn't want to drag him into my personal shit. When it got right down to it, I didn't trust Rocky enough to be honest with him. We were never close that way.

I told him where Adriana was staying, thanked him, and left. I was relieved he didn't pressure me for more information.

It was time to take a ride down to South Broadway. The Swagger In was open early for business.

I parked my car, slid the bat back under the seat, put on a pair of sunglasses, and walked in the front door. It was still pretty early.

Three people were already at the bar, kicking off their day with a daily bottle of their favorite liquid breakfast. Daytime alcoholics are not particular about what time they start drinking. Anytime is good for them.

I walked up to the bar, opened my wallet, laid down a twenty, and sat on the first stool. Everybody at the bar looked at me suspiciously—including the bartender. This was a neighborhood bar, and I was an outsider. The bartender approached and asked what I was having.

"I'll have a Crown Royal on the rocks," I said it like I owned the place. Then I raised my hand in the air with the twenty in hand and shouted, "Drinks for all my friends."

All the early-morning alcohol junkies tipped their bottles in gratitude and went back to minding their business. I sat at the bar all morning waiting for Blondie to show up, but he didn't show. It was too early.

My hope at this point was to catch Blondie alone, off guard, when he least expected it. I wanted a chance to end this whole thing by myself—without getting Rubin involved. But the opportunity wouldn't come.

After two hours, I nodded to the bartender, left a tip, and headed to the men's room. I wanted to check out the layout of the bar.

I knew where the restrooms were. I knew there was a back door. I knew there was a basement door that probably led to a storage area. I knew how big the place was, and I knew how well it was lit. The regulars didn't strike me as any kind of threat. There was no one in the place I needed to be concerned with.

The next time I walked in, I'd be a lot more familiar and comfortable. It was almost like planning a robbery, but all I was really looking for was a tactical advantage.

Who was I kidding? I had no idea who or what I'd be facing. There was no advantage.

CHAPTER 22

I got in my car and drove around the neighborhood for a while. Eventually, I got tired of cruising and parked about fifty feet from the entrance of the bar. I wanted see who came and went. I waited around for almost two more hours, but no bikers showed, neither did Blondie. Maybe he was at the funeral parlor, making arrangements for his motorcycle.

I hoped that Blondie finding his motorcycle totally destroyed would make him feel a little less invincible. I wanted him to know that feeling of vulnerability. I wanted to destroy something he cared about. I wanted Blondie to ponder the mystery of who did it, who got to him. I wanted him to wonder who would do something like that right under his nose, while he slept peacefully in his bed less than fifty feet away. I wanted him to have to consider what someone like that would do next. . . . I wanted to get into his head.

It was closing in on two o'clock—time to pick up Rubin. Driving to the old neighborhood brought back a lot of memories. I began to question the path I was on. It seemed like there was no other choice.

"If it don't feel right, get your ass outta sight." The old man's words kept ringing in my head. I ignored them. I was already wired to drive into the center of the storm. I was being given a chance to settle an old score. It felt like it was meant to be.

I thought about how close I came to death from our last encounter.

Is it all worth it? Damn Right it is.

For somewhere deep inside, the hurt still smoldered. I dismissed my uncomfortable feeling. Mental preparation is important for something like this, and I needed to be ready.

* ⎯⎯ •

When I got to Cherokee and Compton, I saw Rubin standing on the corner. He was shuffling his feet. He saw me from across the street and jogged on up to my car. He jumped in the passenger seat, and said, "I didn't think you'd show."

I looked at Rubin and said. "I knew you would."

Rubin laughed. "I've been thinking long and hard about this, and I've come to the conclusion that you are no longer Bat Man."

"What do you mean?"

"From now on, I'm calling you the Human Torch." We both cracked up.

"Stretch would be proud," Rubin nodded in agreement.

The car grew silent. Memories of Stretch filled my head. Thoughts about his senseless death and what Rubin and I were about to do gave me a forboding sense of apprehension.

Rubin broke the silence. "Stretch would have been here in a heartbeat if he could have been."

Again, silence. Both of us knew the truth of it. There was nothing more to say.

I went into this with the intention of rounding up both Rubin and Stretch. Now there was just me and Rubin. Neither of us had any idea what we would encounter once we found Blondie.

The same questions kept cropping up in my mind: *Who would Blondie be running with? How many of them would there be? What were they carryin'?* There were so many unknowns that I didn't want to think about it anymore.

I remembered the old man's rule: If you don't know, let it go. But I couldn't let it go. I was past the point of thinking. If I saw my opportunity, I was going to leap into it. Now more than ever, I wanted to make this the most unforgettable night of Blondie's life.

It would soon turn out to be the most unforgettable night for all of us.

"Listen, Rubin," I said, breaking the silence. "This is my fight. I don't want you to get involved in this unless somebody other than Blondie jumps in."

Rubin looked at me with the confidence of a maniac and said, "Don't worry, I got this. Come on. Let's go. We don't want to be late. Besides, I've got something on for later tonight."

As we got closer to the Swagger In, I told Rubin about my early-morning field trip and filled him in on what I knew about the bar and the people inside. Rubin listened closely, but he didn't say anything. By the time I finished, we were less than a block away. No motorcycles were parked out front.

"Here we go," I said as I pulled up to a parking space.

Rubin perked up. "I know this place. Let's go in and have a drink. You're buyin."

"So what else is new?"

The crowd was light. We walked up to the bar and parked our asses on the first two stools closest to the front door. We ordered drinks and waited. More customers began to filter in, but still no sign of any bikers.

Ninety minutes later, we heard the first motorcycles pull up. Three One-Eyed Jacks came in and sat at a table. Blondie wasn't one of them. Rubin looked over at me. I could feel his anticipation. I shook my head no. We ordered more drinks and waited. The bar was starting to fill up.

About twenty minutes later, we heard a commotion outside. Whoever was outside didn't come right in. Whoever they were, they were loud and obnoxious.

I was starting to grow impatient. I felt compelled to go out and see who it was.

I looked over at Rubin and said, "I'm going out to the car." I felt like something was winding me up from the inside out. Rubin sensed it as well.

"I'm going with you," Rubin said, as he sprang off the bar stool. Rubin knew if Blondie was outside, I would start this thing without him. He stayed right with me as I walked toward the door.

As we passed through the front entranceway, we came face-to-face with Blondie and another one of the One-Eyed Jacks. I was less than two feet away and he didn't recognize me, but I recognized him. He was the one who came within a hair's breath of taking my life.

Rubin took a hard look at him. It caught Blondie's attention. They stared at each other momentarily. We walked on by and made our way back to the car.

"That's him," I told Rubin. "I'm sure of it. He's the one who robbed me and left me for dead."

I was really jacked up and trying to contain it. I took off my sunglasses and reached under my seat, grabbing the mini-bat.

"Let's go," Rubin said. He was anxious to get in there.

I slid the bat back under the seat and closed the car door.

"What are you doing?" Rubin asked.

"I've waited a long time for this. I'm doin' it without the bat. If you want out, say so right now. I'll understand. This is your last chance to walk away."

Rubin looked at me like I was batshit crazy. "Walk away? Are you fucking kidding me? This is what we came here for!"

Going back in there with no weapons, not knowing what we were up against, was a formula for suicide. I wanted Rubin to have a way out. Leaving the bat in the car was my last-ditch attempt to let him off the hook. I thought he might change his mind and back off at the last minute. That would be the smart thing to do. That's what a sane rational human being would do. But that didn't happen.

Rubin wasn't interested in backing off. At the core of his being, Rubin truly didn't care. I have to confess, at this point, neither did I. Maybe Rubin really did have a death wish. . . . Maybe I did, too.

Rubin was every bit as cranked up and ready as me. It was just what I needed to hear.

"Let's go," I said, as I turned toward the entrance to the bar. Both of us grew silent as we started to make our way back into the bar.

Here we go.

CHAPTER 23

We walked in fast. There was no turning back. The dark forces of anger, resentment, vengeance, and retribution were upon me. Rubin was right behind me.

The Swagger In was crowded. The One-Eyed Jacks were all sitting at the same table. There were five of them. Blondie had his back to me.

Rubin and I moved quickly toward their table. None of them noticed as we approached. They were all involved in conversation. They were completely unaware of our presence or our intentions. I zeroed in on Blondie.

The customers at two other tables noticed as we approached. Their conversation stopped. Somehow, they knew something was about to happen.

"Hey, Blondie," I said. "Turn around." Blondie fucked up. He turned around.

I threw everything I had into a round-house right hook. It caught Blondie across the bridge of his nose. He had just turned around in his chair. I felt his nose snap with the contact.

Blondie flew backwards, head first, over the back of his chair. His hands were covering his face. Blood was flowing through his fingers.

I continued to pound away with no mercy, as the One-Eyed Jacks jumped up from their seats. The table instantly cleared. I picked up a chair and gouged one of the legs into Blondie's ribs. Blondie writhed in pain as two of his crew stood up and drew guns. Rubin shot them both before they could raise their weapons. I was unaware until that moment that Rubin had a gun.

The bar erupted into chaos, as customers scattered in every direction. Tables were being knocked over as people ran for the exits.

I continued to flail away on Blondie with destructive intentions amidst the chaos, the bedlam and the gunfire. More shots rang out. Suddenly, I felt a powerful, crushing blow to my side. Intense, exploding pain burned deep into my stomach. I was shot.

I dropped the chair and collapsed. The impact of the bullet twisted me like a pretzel and instantly took me to the floor. I turned my head to the side. I wanted to see who shot me. It was the bartender.

Rubin stood, unfazed, in the middle of the gunfire. He was shooting back at the bartender. Rubin was now also wounded, but he still kept firing. Rubin shot the bartender twice, once in the shoulder and once in the chest. The bartender fell to the floor behind the bar.

People were crawling on the floor trying to avoid gunfire, while others in a heightened state of panic ran for the exits. The insanity of the moment sucked us in like a magnetic black hole.

Rubin was bleeding from the mouth. He was shot in the chest. Rubin turned his attention to Blondie. He was trying to crawl away.

"Hey, Blondie, where do you think you're goin'?" Rubin stood over Blondie. Rubin was taunting him.

Blondie tried to squirm across the floor. "Hey, look at me!" Rubin shouted once again, but Blondie wouldn't look.

"Hey, Blondie. You don't look so good." Rubin wouldn't let up.

"Hey, Blondie, nothin' down there is gonna help you. You might as well face it. You're fucked."

Rubin kept taunting Blondie, as he tried to squirm across the floor. "Squirm like a worm, you piece-a-shit!" Rubin struggled to follow. They were both moving real slow.

Rubin took a step, aimed his pistol downward, and shot Blondie point blank in the cheek of his ass. Blondie screamed in pain and immediately flipped over. He was lying on the floor, looking up at Rubin. Rubin and Blondie were now face-to-face. Blondie was afraid for his life.

"What's wrong with you, man? I don't even know you," Blondie pleaded. He was looking up at Rubin from the floor with real fear in his eyes.

Rubin was standing directly over Blondie, his gun pointing menacingly at Blondie's chest. "Take a good look at my friend over there on the floor."

Blondie struggled to focus. His nose was smashed in sideways. Blood was still flowing freely from his nostrils. There was a gaping gash on the right side of his cheek that clotted itself closed from the bruising and swelling.

"Do you recognize him?" Rubin asked. Rubin was struggling to breathe.

Blondie turned away. "No, I never saw him before."

"Yes, you have," Rubin said. "You robbed him and threw him in a dumpster to die. Don't you remember?"

Blondie turned his head and looked at me hard. He spit blood from inside his mouth.

"I remember you now. You're Adriana's new savior. You're a fool comin' after me over a whore like that. You should have stayed in that dumpster where you belong—you and that trashy whore girl-friend of yours. I could have saved you a lot of pain and aggravation. That's all that bitch is good for."

"Pain and aggravation is what I came here for you piece-a-shit."

Never before had I felt hatred of this magnitude and intensity. I wanted to finish him once and for all, but I couldn't. I was less than five feet away but I couldn't move. I just laid there, unable to finish what I started.

My stomach was starting to swell. I was bleeding internally. Any move I made shot a sharp, high-voltage pain through my mid-section. It hurt just to breathe. There was nothing I could do but lay there.

Blondie wasn't finished. "You're livin' in a dream world. Adriana is a whore and a drug addict, and nothin' that happens here tonight is ever gonna change that. You think you can win here, but when it's over, you're still going home to a whore and a drug addict."

I waited before I spoke. I wanted to make sure Blondie heard every word of what I had to say.

"Blondie, you're not goin' home. And even if you could, it wouldn't matter. . . . I know where you live."

Blondie's eyes glared at me in hateful recognition. He now knew that I was the one who destroyed his motorcycle.

Blondie was about to say something when Rubin kicked him in the ribs. Blondie curled up into a fetal position. He was desperately gasping for air, trying to catch his breath from Rubin's unexpected kick.

Rubin stood over Blondie and just stared. Rubin's stare was cold—cold, dark, and vacant. He had the eyes of a killer—a killer on a mission. That's what Blondie was facing.

"Rubin," I shouted, "give me the gun!" More than anything, I wanted revenge. But it wouldn't come from me.

Rubin looked over, but he didn't say anything. He could see how bad I was hurt. Blood soaked my clothes from front to back. Deep stabbing pains intensified with every heartbeat. I was dying. I just . . . laid there.

Rubin ignored the fatal wound to his chest. He turned his attention to Blondie. Blondie knew he was doomed. He kept looking away.

"What do you want from me?" Blondie finally said. He still refused to look directly at Rubin. Blondie was afraid to face his fate.

Rubin didn't answer. He just kept staring. It was like he was looking right through Blondie with that cold, dark, empty expression.

After a long silence, Rubin spoke. "Look at me, Blondie. I want you to face the one who's gonna snatch your life away."

Blondie was desperate. Two of his compadres were face down on the floor. Tables and chairs were scattered everywhere over broken glass and the blood-soaked floor. There was an eerie silence now, as the three of us looked at the war zone that was once the Swagger In. I broke the silence.

"Hey, Blondie, take a look at those two pieces a shit on the floor next to you. There's your future. Last night I took your motorcycle apart, and tonight I took you apart. I want you to know—before you go—I loved every second of it."

Blondie turned his head to face me. His eyes still burned with hate. "You're lucky I didn't get to you first. Maybe I'll see you around next time."

I laughed at him. "There is no next time, dumb-ass. You're even dumber than you look." These were my final words to Blondie.

Rubin interrupted. "Well Tex, looks like this is your last hootenanny." Rubin laughed at his own stupid joke.

Blondie finally looked up at Rubin. He must have thought that Rubin had a change of heart. Blondie was wrong. When it came to dealing with Blondie, Rubin didn't have a heart. Rubin's expression instantly turned cold.

"Don't do it!" Blondie pleaded. Blondie knew he was face-to-face with his own personal angel of death. With no warning, Rubin squeezed the trigger and shot Blondie again.

Blondie fell into a dazed stupor. A vacant, glassy-eyed expression came over him. His life was slipping away.

Rubin stared at Blondie for a long time. They were like two dead men staring into their final life-defining moment. Rubin finally spoke.

"Don't worry, Blondie. Death comes to all of us. Sooner or later, everybody takes their turn."

Rubin raised his pistol and pulled the trigger one final time. Blondie died on the floor, begging for his life.

Three more shots rang out. The shots fired came from a police officer. Rubin collapsed in a lifeless heap. The smell of gunpowder and death filled the air. My friend was dead before he hit the floor. Rubin died defending my life. Rubin's final act would be my final revenge.

I looked over at Blondie's two lifeless compadres face-down on the floor. One was wearing dirty, old, beat-to-shit black leather construction boots. I remembered those boots from my first encounter with Blondie. I never saw his face, but I would never forget those boots. Without knowing it, Rubin killed both of my attackers.

CHAPTER 24

The next thing I remember is waking up in a hospital bed in handcuffs. My hands and feet were cuffed on both sides to chrome railings.

I was under arrest for attempted murder, conspiracy to commit murder, first-degree assault, aggravated battery, and illegal use of a deadly weapon—a chair. My rights were read to me, fingerprints were taken, charges were filed, and personal information recorded. Arraignment was delayed because I was considered medically unfit to stand before a judge.

Life as I knew it was over. Rubin was dead. Blondie was dead. The bartender was dead. The two One Eyed Jacks that Rubin shot— both dead. I learned this from the doctor who saved my life.

I asked the doctor why he saved my life. He looked at me, but he didn't answer. . . .

The next face I saw was a police officer. He said I was facing life in prison. He wanted to take my statement and get my side of the story. He said if I cooperated, I might get a better deal. I wasn't interested in a better deal. I told him I couldn't remember anything.

The police officer wasn't finished. He had a question he wanted to ask. "Five people are dead because of you. How do you feel about that?"

I don't remember exactly what I said. I was pretty drugged up. But I'm pretty sure I said, "Go fuck yourself."

The next time I woke up, I was looking at the face of my brother. He was standing at the foot of my bed. He said our mother passed away. He said our mother's death was my fault. She saw the whole shooting incident unwind on the evening news. When she heard that Rubin and I were involved, she collapsed from an apparent heart attack in her living room in front of the TV. My brother found her lying lifeless on the floor. He tried to revive her, but it was too late. She was pronounced dead on the scene by the city coroner and taken away.

I wouldn't be able to attend the funeral. I would be in custody in the hospital. I would never see my mother again. I would never be able to set things right between us. I would never get the chance to tell her how much I loved her.

My brother wasn't finished. He went to Casa Roma to break the news about the shooting and my mother's passing to Adriana. As he knocked on the door, he could hear the TV, but Adriana didn't answer. He knew something was wrong and summoned the motel manager.

The motel manager and my brother found Adriana lying on the bed. At first they thought she was sleeping. A small trickle of blood running from her left nostril was the only indication that her heart had stopped.

Police and paramedics were called, but there was nothing they could do. They found a single needle track in her arm and a used syringe in the trash can. A newspaper beside her had a front-page headline that read, "Five People Slain in Local Tavern Massacre." The article named me as one of the shooting victims and went on to describe eyewitness accounts of the deadly attack and gunfight that led to the death of five people. Adriana died from an apparent heroin overdose—probably a short time after reading the article. I would never see my beautiful Adriana again.

My brother finished by saying I was dead to him. "Don't call, don't write. If you ever get out of jail and see me on the street, just walk away and I'll do the same." Those were his final words to me. I never saw or spoke to my brother again.

In one out-of-control moment, I destroyed everybody I cared about. I cursed the God I didn't believe in. But more than that, I cursed myself for still being alive.

Why did I live through this?

I wept for my mother. She was completely innocent of any of this, and yet my actions indirectly ended her life. I cried for Adriana. All I wanted was to give her a better life, and now I felt responsible for ending it. I once told her I would never put my heart out there for someone who couldn't do the same, but deep down, I loved her with all my heart, and now she was gone, my heart was broken.

I cried for Rubin. I hadn't seen him in years, and yet still, after all that time, he stood by my side and watched over me, right to the very end. Rubin died defending my life. I couldn't bear the guilt. I used him because I needed him, and now, because of me, he was dead.

Six people were shot that day, and out of all of them, I was the only one left alive.

Why was I still here?

More than anything, I wanted to be the One-Eyed Jacks' worst nightmare, and now the nightmare had come to me as well. The hurt and loss I felt descended on me like a continuous form of nonstop torture. Waves of guilt and remorse washed over me like an endless ocean of anguish. There was no end to it.

Hell is not some inferno you go to after you die. It's right here, waiting for you twenty-four-seven, and there's no escape.

I felt a deep sense of guilt and remorse in every fiber of my being. An emotional breakdown was in progress. I was in a downward spiral fueled by guilt, remorse, and my desire for self-punishment. Physical tremors erupted into a deep inner quake. I was now held captive by forces I didn't fully understand.

How it all happened, the way it happened, the ugliness of the whole situation, the all of it—all seemed to begin and end with me.

There's no escape. Death would be a welcome relief.

I begged the doctors to end my life. I was totally broken. "Just kill me now," I pleaded.

Never before had I felt emotional pain of this magnitude. Never before had I felt so alone.

———

The next thing I knew, I was bound face up in a hospital bed. Leather straps tightly secured my hands and feet. I was in an isolation cell, looking out of a thick glass window. A guard stood outside, staring at me through the glass.

I was being monitored in a suicide-watch room. Shortly after my surgery from the gunshot wound, a nurse found me unconscious in the recovery room, lying in a pool of blood in my hospital bed.

The doctors would later describe it, as a gaping abdominal wound that had been ripped open, leaving my internal organs exposed. An uncontrolled bleed spilled out on to the bed sheets. Apparently I found a way to rip open my abdominal stitches.

An emergency surgical team was called in to repair the damage caused by me forcibly reopening my abdominal cavity. To this day I have no memory of the actual act.

The surgeons who operated on me went to great lengths to save my life—a second time. A portion of my intestines were removed. Repairs were made to my colon and liver, while internal bleeding and acute infection remained as the primary obstacles I was facing.

I was a far cry from being out of the woods, but the physical pain was nothing compared to the inner torture that forced its way into my consciousness.

My arraignment would again be delayed. A complete psychological examination would be ordered to determine whether I was fit to stand trial.

So off to the nut house I went. . . .

CHAPTER 25

Once I was healthy enough, I was transported by ambulance to a state-funded mental health institution in the St. Louis area. A corrections officer was assigned to ride along during my transport.

Upon arrival, I was once again taken to a suicide-watch room. Again, I was strapped face up by my wrists and ankles to a bed in a small, empty room with one door and a large, thick-glass observation window. A uniformed guard regularly monitored my condition from the other side of the glass.

I was now a prisoner of the state. My life, and my decisions regarding my life, were no longer my own. It was the ultimate frustration and the ultimate liberation all at the same time. There was nothing I had to do, nowhere I had to be except right where I was. I couldn't drink when I was thirsty. I couldn't eat when I was hungry. I couldn't even wipe my own ass. Life inside is one big nothing.

Eventually, a doctor came in to see me. He asked me many questions. I had nothing to say. He explained that cooperation works best in circumstances like this. He said I was in this position for my own good.

I interrupted him in mid-sentence. "Goodness," I said, "has nothing to do with this." He seemed pleased that he got a response from me.

He asked me why I ripped my stitches out. I said I had no memory of doing any such thing. It was a true statement. I didn't remember.

The doctor then asked, "Why do you think you're here?"

"I'm here for the delicious gourmet food and the outstanding personal services rendered by this fine institution."

He ignored my remark and said, "I'll be back tomorrow. If you want to work our program, maybe some improvements can be made."

"I want no part of your program, your God, or your solutions."

He turned, looked at me, and said, "Sooner or later, you'll change your mind. I'm the only game in town." Then he walked out of the room.

This was obviously not the doctor's first rodeo. I had to admit it. He was right. I had no other options. My life was over. Sleep was my only escape. But what do you do when even sleep, your only place of refuge, is invaded by the dark dream?

It all started with the closing of my eyes. . . .

Even before I close them, I know he's there, waiting. And from deep within the darkness springs a presence. I can't see him, but I can feel him looking at me. I have no idea who he is, but his presence is powerful. He sees right through me. His eyes pierce my heart.

I turn in desperation, only to find myself at the edge—the edge of the ledge. I was standing at the edge of a deep, dark chasm. And looking down into a boundless pit of darkness, I know there's nowhere left to run.

A booming voice like my father's spoke to me from out of nowhere. . .

"The darkness you face is your own. There is no dark force of anger. There is no dark force of resentment. There is no dark force of vengeance. There is no dark force of retribution!"

The voice continues:

"How long will you run from the truth and the light?

When will you find the courage to face the reality?

You are responsible. You are to blame.

Turning from truth and turning from God are one and the same."

It was the booming voice of truth.

I woke up in a cold sweat. Maybe I am fucking crazy. Maybe I'm right where I belong.

———

I stayed awake all night, contemplating the meaning of the dream. One thing was certain: I didn't have all the answers. As a matter of fact, I didn't have any answers. Here I was, strapped to a bed in an isolated holding cell in the nut house.

Maybe some self-analysis is warranted. Maybe a different attitude is called for. It was once again time to eat my cornflakes and shut the fuck up.

Daybreak was a welcome event. It ushered in a whole new attitude. I was exhausted from the previous dark-night-of-the-soul-self-analysis. I was tired of being restrained and anxious to talk to the doctor.

By late morning, he stopped by to check on me.

"So, how are you feeling today?" he asked.

"I've been lying here, crucified to this bed, for more than ten days. How do you expect me to feel?"

"I'll make a deal with you," the doctor said. "If you promise you won't hurt yourself or anybody else, I'll have those restraints removed. What do you say?"

I agreed. The doctor had security remove my restraints.

Although I was free of the restraints, I was far from free. I was moving slowly, still healing from the gunshot wound to my abdomen. It felt good just to be able to turn over in bed.

I was moved to a room with a toilet, a shower, and sink—what wonderful inventions! I cupped my hands under the running water and drank.

The next two days were spent drinking water from the tap, sleeping, and eating meals delivered on stainless-steel trays. Taking a shower was a luxury beyond luxuries.

Later in the week, my doctor told me I would soon be allowed to join the rest of the patients being treated on the floor. He warned me that this was a locked ward, and that any attempts to leave or escape would result in disciplinary action.

"Trust," he said, was the main link in the chain of the doctor-patient relationship.

"I hope you won't betray that trust."

I said, "not to worry. I have nowhere else to go."

He started to leave, but as he walked away, I stopped him with a question. "Hey Doc, how come you're allowing me to roam free to interact with the other patients?"

"Because aside from your assault, you show no history of violence. I've read your case file and reviewed the police reports. I don't believe you're violent by nature." With that, he walked away.

I was now free to roam the floor. I was still a little unstable on my feet. It was time to start moving. *Taking a short walk might be good for me.*

I left my room and proceeded slowly down the corridor. I had never been in the nut house before. I wondered what it was like to mingle with crazy people.

As I walked down the hallway, I came to a small reception area with a nursing station. Artificial plants in plastic pots were positioned in front of unbreakable, maximum-security-windows. I could only suppose they were placed there to enhance the illusion that light was somehow a necessity for their survival.

Several soft, heavily padded chairs were strategically positioned in front of a television. A mild-mannered, middle-age lady wearing a flowered bathrobe sat there watching *The Price Is Right*. I sat down next to her and introduced myself.

"How are you? My name is Roman. Do you mind if I sit here?"

"Go right ahead. I'm Edna."

"Nice to meet you, Edna. So how long have you been here?"

"Going on my fourth week. I'm starting to get frustrated. I don't belong here."

"I know what you mean, Edna. I haven't been here nearly as long as you, and it's starting to get to me, too."

Edna went on. "What bothers me the most is that they treat me like I'm some sort of criminal."

"What do you mean?"

"They accused me of arson."

"Oh my, that's terrible! How could they possibly accuse you of something like that?"

"That's what I said. First, they accused me of setting the garbage dumpster at the back of my house on fire. Then they blamed me for my husband's car catching fire. Then they arrested me when my neighbor's garage caught fire! I was fit to be tied!"

Edna went on. "Before I knew it, I found myself under arrest and charged with arson. I still can't believe it.

"It all happened so fast. Before I knew it, they locked me up and left me all alone in this filthy little isolated holding cell with no TV and no one to talk to. And wouldn't you know it, the next thing you know my mattress catches on fire. Can you believe it? They tried to blame that on me, too!"

"That's quite a story, Edna," I said, looking at the clock. "Oh my, look at the time. You'll have to excuse me. I have some business I have to attend to."

I eased myself out of my chair. "It was really nice meeting you, Edna. I hope everything works out for you."

"Nice meeting you too, Roman. I hope we can talk again soon."

"I'm looking forward to it. You take care of yourself."

Poor Edna. I hope someone here can help her.

As I walked down another corridor, I heard the sound of classical music. I wasn't a big classical music fan, but something about the music struck a familiar chord. When I got to the TV room, I understood why. It was a Bugs Bunny cartoon.

Nobody noticed as I made my way into the room. They were all "zombied out," mesmerized into a chemically altered vegetative state with an effective combination of thorazine and Looney Tunes.

I sat down and watched with great interest. It had been years since I watched cartoons, but this one I remembered. It was a real classic.

It's the one where Bugs is playin' the banjo, and his playin' gets on the nerves of this highfalutin opera singer who thinks his shit don't stink. I never could understand it. How could any bona fide music lover not appreciate the banjo? Anyway, finally—at his wit's end, in a fit of rage, the opera singer demolishes Bugs Bunny's banjo. Well, needless to say, Bugs messes with this guy for the rest of the cartoon. But it's the clever way he goes about it that really gets you!

On the night of the opera singer's grand performance, Bugs disguises himself as Leopold, the famous conductor, and the disguise works to a T. Dressed in a full tux, tails, and a wig—so no one recognizes him—he walks on stage and captures the audience with his mere presence.

A quiet hush falls over the audience. The silence grows. The tension mounts as Leopold prepares to bring the house down. He waits for the right moment, takes the baton, snaps it in two, and tosses it aside with an air of total confidence. You see, the baton's not expressive enough.

Leopold uses his hands to conduct.

In the silence of the moment, I scan the room, when it occurs to me that loony tunes are watchin' Looney Tunes! It struck me kind of funny, so I started to laugh. But the more I thought about it, the more it started to bother me.

You see, sitting there, staring at my droned-out, dead-headed compadres,

I understood maybe for the first time just exactly what these bastards were doing to us. . . . This wasn't treatment. This was vegetable management! It made me really angry.

I jumped out of my chair and shouted, "What's goin' on here? This is bullshit!"

Just so you know, raging comments and accusations are not well received in mental institutions. The "help" quickly responded to my outburst. I was restrained once again and given a heavy dose of a sedative I now refer to as "instant cooperation." The whole confrontation lasted about twenty seconds.

As the drug-induced fog descended, I found myself in a new confrontation. It was me against the drug, and the drug was winning.

My desperation quickly grew to frenzy, but still I refused to let those bastards see my panic or my pain. That's when I heard the music. From out of nowhere, it was coming from the TV. With all my strength, I raised my head, and standing there, like a pillar of strength, was the master maestro himself—Leopold! And he was conducting his ass off!

As the intensity of the music increased, so did my strength. Buildings shook! Walls rattled! As the master maestro brought both the orchestra and audience to the brink of hypnotic frenzy. I continued to hold on. Suddenly, I realized that under that stiff outer appearance of Leopold was another bona fide lunatic—just like me!

There we were the two of us, Leopold and I, both feverishly fighting to demolish the confines of this so-called well-established institution. I continued to hold on. Tears of gratitude came as I inwardly thanked my unexpected ally who came to my aid in a time and place where I previously thought I was alone. It was almost as if we formed some sort of bond—some spiritual alliance—both of us united by the one common purpose of bringing the house down. It was us against them.

I continued to hold on.

Leopold continued to push the performance to a feverish pitch. The momentum of the music erupted to the point where the building shattered and crumbled. The audience cheered and applauded.

At last, the walls were broken. . . . I continued to hold on.

Once again, I was struck with a sudden flash of unexpected insight—like a mental hand grenade exploding with the sudden force and fury that brings not only expansion but vision and clarity to an otherwise dull set of senses.

It was all so clear now. To bring the house down. . . . That's what everybody wants. . . . We want the earth to move. . . . We want the ground to shake. . . . We want our walls to crumble. . . . We want our cages rattled—to be moved, swept off our feet, seduced by the sound, mesmerized by the magic of the moment. . . . I continued to hold on.

The cartoon was much more than just a cartoon. It was a message: Don't be afraid. It's OK. Let the walls crumble.

It's all a part of your grand performance.

Now I understood. . . . The drug was starting to dominate. . . So hard to hold on. . . . Just a little longer. . . . Consciousness . . . slipping . . . away. . . .

Thank you, Leopold. . . . Thank you for being there. . . . Thank you for breaking the barriers. . . . Thank you for showing me the way.

CHAPTER 26

Once again, I woke up in restraints. Antipsychotic drugs are obviously not my thing.

My doctor was standing at my bedside. "Roman, what happened in the TV room?"

"I flipped out."

"What do you mean, 'you flipped out'?"

"I can't explain it. Being in here is no walk in the park. I had a kind of revelation."

"What kind of revelation?"

"The kind of revelation that made me realize I want to get the fuck out of here as soon as possible. I don't care if I go straight to jail. If you're the only game in town, I'm ready to play."

"I'm curious. What changed your attitude?"

"This place changed my attitude!"

The doctor started to laugh. "This place has motivated many individuals to seek positive solutions to their problems. I'm glad to see you come around. Why don't we start by removing your restraints. Are you OK with that?"

"Absolutely."

It was time to open the lines of communication. During the next few days, I told Doc my story. I told him about my previous run-in with Blondie and how my relationship with my now-deceased girlfriend brought the two of us back together. I told him about the guilt I suffered from the loss of so many people I cared about.

I said I was glad Blondie was dead, but if I could do it all over again, I would do it differently. I also told Doc that I was sorry for putting so many innocent bystanders in danger and subjecting them to such a traumatic situation. I said I was angry, scared, careless, and out of control, and I was glad more innocent people didn't get hurt.

Doc listened patiently to my story. He took a moment before speaking. "You're ready to go to court," he said, and then he darted out of the room.

Another week went by before my scheduled arraignment proceedings. Once again, a corrections officer escorted me to my destination. I was transported in restraints to the city courthouse for my hearing. There was no jury. This was a hearing with my public defender, the judge, and the city prosecutor to determine whether I was fit to stand trial. The only other people in the room were a court stenographer, a bailiff, and a police officer who could be called to testify.

Once we got started, my lawyer leaped into action. He was quick to point out to the judge that every victim who died that day died from gunshot wounds. He followed up by pointing out that I did not have a gun and never fired a shot. He cited the statements of firsthand witnesses, all of whom identified Rubin as the shooter.

My lawyer claimed I was forced to participate in an egregious act. He went on to say that I was more afraid of Rubin than Austin Agoria. He further explained my previous association with Austin and Austin's previous association with Adriana.

He stated that both Rubin and Agoria had criminal histories, drug histories, and violent histories, and often intimidated individuals into complying with their demands.

My attorney was painting a convincing picture for the judge implicating Rubin as the fall guy. As he continued, it looked more and more like I was a tragic victim caught up in Rubin's murderous assault. I would have none of it!

I could no longer stand to listen to my lawyer blame everything on Rubin. Rubin died looking out for me, and I wasn't going to allow this guy to crucify him like that.

I told my lawyer I wanted to speak to the court on my own behalf. He advised me against taking the stand, but I *insisted*. It was time to get to the truth.

After I was sworn in, the judge asked me one question. "What motivated you to attack Mr. Austin Agoria?"

I began by defending Rubin from my lawyer's accusations.

"Your Honor, I would like to say before the court that the assault on Austin was my intention right from the start. My lawyer stated that Rubin recruited me, when in fact *I recruited Rubin*. Rubin's only purpose was to back me up. I entered the Swagger In intent on revenge for the assault and robbery that Austin inflicted on me years ago. I almost died from the injuries.

"I also wanted to make Austin pay for the terror and anguish that he regularly subjected my girlfriend to.

"I've heard my lawyer state that I was a victim caught up in Rubin's murderous assault. Nothing could be further from the truth. Rubin's actions were in my defense. He died delivering justice for me. The incident escalated because I caused it to escalate. I would also like to say with great conviction, if I wouldn't have gotten shot, I would have killed Austin myself."

My lawyer was not happy with my testimony. He quickly followed up with a closing argument. He stated that I was not of right mind when faced with a sudden confrontation with the alleged victim and should not be prosecuted or incarcerated in any institution unless I was deemed to be of right mind by a qualified, licensed psychiatrist. He cited my previous suicide attempt in the hospital as proof that I was unfit to stand trial.

I couldn't believe what I was hearing from my lawyer. I just finished explaining under oath, and with great accuracy, the exact motivations of my actions on that day. I knew exactly what I was doing and why I was doing it. I couldn't believe what was coming out of my lawyer's mouth. Never before did I feel more right about anything!

The prosecutor for the state strongly objected to allowing testimony from a psychiatrist. He argued that my testimony was nothing short of a confession. I strongly agreed! He further argued that I knew exactly what I was doing when I launched the attack at the Swagger In. I strongly agreed!

The prosecutor went on to state that I willfully and intentionally sought out Austin Agoria for the sole purpose of seeking revenge. Again, I strongly agreed with the prosecutor!

The prosecutor argued passionately that I should be prosecuted to the full extent of the law. Again, I agreed with him 100 percent!

The prosecutor also stated that I showed no remorse whatsoever for the killing of Austin Agoria. He argued that maximum sentences were warranted. Again, I had to agree!

To make a long story short, the judge agreed with my lawyer. Either the judge completely ignored the fact that I sided with the prosecution, or he believed I *really was crazy* for making no attempt to defend myself.

Despite my protest, the judge ordered a full and complete psychological examination given to determine and evaluate the quality of my mental status. A psychiatrist would be allowed to give testimony on my behalf.

It was almost as if my testimony was being ignored. Strange forces were at work here. I was attempting to convict myself, and it wasn't being allowed.

The prosecutor about blew a gasket!

How much crazier could things possibly get?

CHAPTER 27

My psychiatrist was called to the stand. He began by stating his credentials and years of experience. After he finished giving the details of his education and work history, he launched into the start of my defense.

"Your Honor," he said, "I gave the defendant an extensive in-depth psychological examination and review. I've also read police reports and conducted many in-depth interviews with the defendant. I'm familiar with his history and background, and I've reviewed extensively all the pertinent facts and relevant information regarding this case.

"After my examination and review, I see no reason for the defendant to be incarcerated."

He paused to ensure that his opening had its intended effect on the judge, the prosecutor, and my attorney.

"Your Honor," he continued, "the defendant has no prior arrests and no history of any illegal activity. Before this event, he was a productive member of society, involved in a stable relationship with an unblemished work record. Although he has expressed no regret or remorse for the death of Austin Agoria, he has demonstrated deep regret and remorse for the outcome of the events that unfolded on that deadly night in question."

I listened to my psychiatrist's testimony with unwavering attention.

"The defendant's actions, Your Honor, were understandable from a psychological perspective considering the overall circumstances. I believe the defendant when he says that he had no prior knowledge of the concealed weapon used in the shooting death of the bartender, Austin Agoria, and the two assailants who died on the scene.

"The defendant's portrayal of the events of that evening is supported not only by witnesses, but also by pictures of both assailants, who died at the scene at their table with guns in their hands. Further, his explanation for his actions has a clear ring of truth. I would also like to point out that the defendant was equally open, candid, and spontaneous during his analysis and evaluation."

Doc continued his testimony. "The defendant's behavior on that horrific night fit the behavior of an animal trapped into defending his offspring. It's of great importance to note here that any human being who endures the stress and anguish associated with a life-threatening encounter could easily regress to this kind of behavior.

"Your Honor, I would respectfully ask the court to keep in mind that before this incident, the defendant demonstrated no threat to society. In view of his work history and his lack of a prior arrest history, I am confident that he can function normally in society and will pose no threat to himself or others.

"He took no deadly actions, Your Honor, and the personal stress and strain resulting from his previous encounter with Mr. Austin Agoria explains his behavior.

"Finally, in view of the personal losses that resulted directly or indirectly from the defendant's actions, it is my opinion, Your Honor, that he has suffered enough."

My lawyer closed by restating the opinion of my psychiatrist. "Your Honor, incarceration would only further poison the life of an innocent man who has already suffered immeasurable losses."

To make a long story short, the judge agreed with my lawyer and psychiatrist. He ordered my release with time served. The judge ruled that I was to continue therapy and that the court would monitor my progress.

Holy shit! I couldn't believe it! The judge is setting me free! I've somehow escaped prosecution!

The prosecutor again went ballistic! He cited verbatim my sworn testimony and the subsequent confession I gave on the witness stand. He accused the judge of sending a "self-proclaimed murderer" back on the street and threatened to file a formal complaint against the judge. "Allowing the defendant to return to society is an act of gross negligence by the court," he declared.

The judge held the prosecutor in contempt and fined him two thousand dollars!

The day after I was released, the prosecutor committed suicide.

He arrived at his office, told his secretary to hold all calls, closed his office door, and sat down behind his desk. He then removed a snub-nosed thirty-eight caliber revolver from the top right-hand drawer of his desk, put the pistol to his temple, and blew his brains out.

The prosecuting attorney apparently suffered from acute depression resulting from a long string of courtroom losses. My case supposedly pushed him over the edge. The joke amongst his peers was that he couldn't even get a conviction against a defendant who confessed under oath on the witness stand. Because of my case, he became the laughing stock of the prosecutor's office. The humiliation of losing a slam-dunk conviction against a defendant who literally begged to be convicted was apparently more than he could take.

How crazy is that!

———

I was once again free—but not really. I returned to my studio, where remnants of Adriana's clothes were scattered in haste from our previous departure. Standing in the quiet emptiness of the studio, I broke down. My actions on that fateful night led to the death of seven people. There was no escape from that.

I moved from bar to bar, from place to place in search of anything that would take me away from the ugliness and the emptiness. I sought out old friends and familiar faces in search of just a few moments of companionship—maybe even a decent conversation—but none of it was working. All I could think of was Adriana, Rubin, my mother, and the events that had gone so horribly wrong.

I began to feel more and more isolated, a downward spiral was starting to escalate. My only friend now was the alcohol. It was the last and only cushion I had left and the only thing that never changed. It was the only thing left I could really count on.

I was haunted. Haunted by the absence of Adriana. Haunted by the absence of Rubin. Haunted by the absence of my mother. Haunted by guilt, remorse, anger and loneliness. Once again, a downward spiral was taking hold. Part of me knew it, the other part didn't care.

I was angry, drunk, wounded, and out of control. People were avoiding me now. It was as if I crossed some kind of line, and everyone I came into contact with knew it. It was a line between the caring and the uncaring, the responsible and the irresponsible, the sane and the insane. What they were witnessing frightened them, and they all knew instinctively to stay away.

How I got to where I was no longer mattered. I was far beyond the point of caring. What happened from that point on is really foggy. . . .

CHAPTER 28

I remember waking up in handcuffs. I was in a vacant lot in East St. Louis. I was once again arrested or in protective custody. Four days had passed, though I could recall only two.

My only memory of the previous four days was that I tried to reconnect with a past that was no longer there. The bar that once stood there was obviously gone. Not even a building remained. Weeds and trash were the only markers left to recount my outdated memory.

I was chasing ghosts—long-dead memories of the past. That's all I had left. I was broke, friendless, hungry, cold, under arrest, and—worst of all—out of alcohol.

The police removed my handcuffs, and emergency personnel took me away on a stretcher.

The attendants loaded me on to an ambulance. "Take me away," I shouted. "Take me away."

The ambulance ride was smooth and quiet as I rested on the comfort of clean paper sheets. The only discomfort I felt came from the ambulance attendant, who was nervously busy writing out his report. He seemed uneasy with my presence.

Maybe it's because I'm a wandering, drunk, disgusting, out-of-control derelict. Maybe that has something to do with it.

I wanted only to sleep, but my mind wouldn't let me. For some reason, the attendant's uneasiness reminded me of the uneasiness of the people I encountered in the last two days. They were people I always thought of as friends, some of them good friends—brothers of the night who delighted themselves in a lifestyle similar to mine. I could see their faces in my mind and how visibly shaken they were by my presence. Some of them pretended not to see me, some pretended not to know me, some avoided me altogether, and some just plain ran away.

What was it besides my disgusting demeanor that frightened them so?

I laid there vacant, waiting for an answer, and that's when it hit me. What they saw in me was a speeded-up version of themselves. The only difference between their self-destructive tendencies and mine was the fact that I was no longer hiding it. With me there was no more pretense.

My delirious downfall was rapidly accelerated by the fact that I was no longer afraid of the free fall. My friends were witness to a kind of futuristic vision of themselves, and watching it scared the living shit out of them.

I think there's some rebellious sense of satisfaction that goes along with an I-don't-care attitude. It's a calmness of spirit that comes with the certainty of your direction. You're going straight into the toilet, and you know it.

It was just like the old man used to say: "Downhill is always faster than uphill." When I was young, he often used that statement as a warning. At the time, it used to really bother me, but it always made me think. Now, I truly didn't care. At least now I was free to enjoy the free fall. A crash landing was now acceptable.

I felt strangely calm, although at the time I didn't know why. It seemed to make little difference to the ambulance attendant sitting next to me. He appeared to be anything but calm. His nervousness fueled my curiosity.

Unlike my friends, he was a complete stranger. I had no feelings about him, good or bad, none whatsoever. And yet, somehow, I knew he felt threatened.

There's another dimension to I-don't-care that creates an uneasiness within the atmosphere. It's a kind of unstable, unpredictable insanity that threatens everyone who comes in contact with it. There's nothing more unpredictable and dangerous than someone with nothing to lose.

The ambulance attendant sat silently next to me, his face still buried in his report. It was obvious by his unwillingness to make eye contact that he was intimidated. I wanted to break the silence, but I wasn't sure how.

"Boo!" I screamed in dramatic fashion at the top of my lungs.

The attendant about jumped out of his seat. His seat belt was the only thing that kept him from banging his head against the roof of the ambulance. Paperwork flew in every direction, as the attendant attempted to recover. I laughed so hard I cried.

The attendant didn't think it was so funny. He glared at me and continued to gather himself along with his paperwork.

The ambulance driver called back, "Everything OK back there?"

He was laughing too.

The attendant, now angry and still somewhat shaken, replied, "Yea, everything's fine."

I took this opportunity to apologize. "Hey, listen. I'm sorry. I shouldn't have scared you like that. I promise I won't do it again."

The attendant nodded to acknowledge my apology but immediately went back to ignoring me. I could tell he was still pissed. I broke the silence one more time.

"Hey, do you know what I'm looking for?" I asked.

"What?" he answered. He was still angry and a bit nervous. He refused to look at me and continued to focus on his paperwork.

"Hey, look at me!" I shouted.

The attendant lowered his paperwork. He was clearly annoyed. It was obvious that he didn't like me.

"What do you want?" He was still really angry and trying to contain it.

"I want a smooth ride home. That's all I'm lookin' for—a smooth ride home. That's all I want."

"You're the boss," he said, looking away once again. "You're the boss."

I wanted to lighten things up. I said I was more of an Elvis fan than a Springsteen fan, but he didn't get the joke. He was still pissed.

I was starting to get annoyed as well. *What's wrong with this guy? Why is he acting like he has a stick up his ass?*

Hey, sorry to interrupt you, but I have just one more question.

What's that?

In all the years that you've worked on an ambulance, what's the most obnoxious disgusting odor you've ever encountered?

Why do you ask?

I didn't answer verbally. I farted instead.

I have to say, it was really disgusting. I couldn't have been more proud.

The ambulance attendant looked like he was about to throw up. I watched as his face changed from anger, to pure misery, to gravely ill. That's when I realized there are no windows that you can open in the back of an ambulance. The attendant had no other choice than to sit there and live with it.

I couldn't help myself. I just had to fuck with him.

"Now you know what it's like to die in the gas chamber."

The attendant covered his nose and mouth with a handkerchief and told the driver to pull over.

The ambulance pulled over and came to a sudden stop. I looked out the back window and saw nothing but dark, empty highway. The ambulance driver got out and opened the double back doors of the ambulance.

"Jesus Christ," he exclaimed, backing away from the back of the ambulance. He pulled his shirt over his nose.

"Jesus Christ can't help you." I answered.

The attendant unstrapped me from the stretcher and said, "get out."

I thought I misunderstood him. "What's this about?" I asked.

"Get out," the attendant repeated.

I couldn't believe it. I was being thrown out of the ambulance. They were leaving me on the gravel roadside of a dark, empty highway.

Anyway, I jumped out of the back of the rig and heard the attendant pick up the microphone and announce, "Returning in service. Patient has exited the ambulance."

I hollered back, "Elvis has exited the ambulance—you assholes!"

They drove off laughing.

Touché

CHAPTER 29

There were no smooth rides left. I was alone, stranded on a dark, lonely highway. It was a metaphor for my life. This was no longer funny.

There was no turning back. There was nothing I could do to erase the tragedy I caused. It didn't matter how much I drank. It didn't matter what form of self-medication I took. The reality of it was always there—waiting. That's the problem with reality. No matter how hard you try to escape, it's always *right there*, waiting.

I started walking. Every once in a while, a car would pass. Sometimes I would try to hitch a ride, but nobody would stop. It all felt so pointless. I had no place to go. I was lost in fatigue, depression, confusion and the devastation of great loss. I stopped and looked up into the dark night sky. Not one star in the sky was visible.

I screamed up to the heavens, "Is that all you got for me? Why don't you just hit me with a truck and get it over with?" I got no response. I wasn't surprised.

Off in the distance, an abandoned car came into view on the side of the road. I was totally and completely washed out. I wanted a place to lay down. Sleep would be a welcome relief. I walked up to the car to open the door.

Maybe I can fall asleep in the back seat. Please be open.

As I grabbed the door handle, I saw my reflection in the window. I stared at my reflection for a long time. I was somehow transported back to a long-lost memory. It was a memory I somehow pushed out of my mind as a young kid.

I was walking home from school, and on the corner of Spring and Wyoming, right in front of the laundromat, a crowd gathered in the street. Now a crowd in the street after school in South St. Louis could mean only one thing and that was a fight. So me being the curious South-sider that I was compelled to stroll on over to see if it was anybody that I knew. I jostled and side-stepped my way to the front of the crowd, but when I got there, I didn't find what I expected.

What I found when I got there was this old man who had been hit by a car. He was lying face up in the street, and he was hurt really bad. His body was all twisted and contorted, and you could see he was all broke-up, because he was bent in places where you're not supposed to bend. He was bleeding from the mouth and breathing real shallow, like any movement of any kind was real painful. And in the intensity of that tired old face, you could see the desperation of a life-and-death struggle.

The crowd tried to encourage him to hang on as best they could, but he paid them no mind. Whatever fight he was in was personal. We all just stood there helpless, watching, real quiet, while the old man stared at the scrambled condition of his own helplessness. He never once said a word, not even in the end. He just watched, as if consciousness was the only thing he had left to hang on to.

It was then that I saw it, in that last look—right there! In that blink-of-an-eye instant right before he let go. It was there that I saw just how much his life meant to him. Then he just relaxed, and it was over.

It was that last look that I'll never forget. When I saw it, I just froze, but it was too late. There was nothing I could do but watch him die. And now, I live with the memory of that one last look.

·————————·

When I came out of it, I was staring back at my own reflection of that one last look. But this time, it was *my* face in the window of an old, abandoned car. . . . The old man's face and mine were one and the same. I was just as lost, just as afraid, just as helpless, just as alone. . . .

And then there was nothing . . . just an empty, cold darkness followed by the loneliest feeling I ever felt. There was no spirit left. The darkness now seemed peaceful, but I was far from being at peace.

So many scars, I thought looking now like a spectator at the lifeless reflection of myself reflected in the window of an old abandoned car. I looked so strange in this current lifeless state. . . . *And then came the darkness . . . that took me back . . . back to old aggressions . . . deep depressions . . . and long-since-forgotten indiscretions. . .*

Like a puppet on a string, danced around at the mercy of my own emotions. That's how I saw myself: enslaved by an identity that ran my life. One by one, past-life images flashed before me in a nonstop cycle of repetitive display—like eternal mental markers of a past never to be erased. And somewhere, buried deep within the reincarnated ruins of a troubled past, a lost soul searches for asylum. . . .

But there is no light, there is no escape. And as the frightened, lost soul begins to drink in the darkness, he starts to panic. It's blacker than black! And slowly, as the darkness begins to devour, there's only the sound of a pounding heart that keeps him from falling into the eternal emptiness.

His chest is ready to explode! The blood rushes in anticipation, as he desperately tries to escape the all-encompassing blackness. . . .

The truth is, I invited the dark forces into my life—opened the doors and allowed their venom to course through my veins and contaminate my soul, fueled them with the chemical forces of drugs and the liquid fire of alcohol. Then it stung me like a bee and poisoned my whole life. It was the direction of my choosing. There was no one to blame but myself.

There's got to be a better way!

I called out in desperation, "Please, God, help me escape from this darkness." And then there was nothing.

•———————•

When I came to, I found myself lying in the gravel, looking up into the dark night sky. And there it was, from seemingly out of nowhere, one single star pierced its way through the thick, liquid darkness. I was lying on my back, looking up in amazement at the beauty and wonder of a living presence that somehow revealed itself.

One star projected like a laser through the dark and peaceful emptiness. It was as if that single, laser-like ray of light somehow lit the whole universe. I pondered how a single, laser-like ray of light could dispel such immense darkness. I was witnessing something extraordinary. . . .

I laid there in peace, and a vision came upon me, off in the distance. It was a face. . . . It was *my* face!

Time to face the face.

I looked with almost childlike wonder at a face I could only recognize as my own. And yet, it seemed so different. It was my face alright, but it was untouched, unscarred, almost lighted, or so it seemed, by an unobstructed energy. And it seemed as if to float, weightless, like an eagle on an updraft.

I was face-to-face with a *heightened version* of myself. This self truly was a king—a king who knew the boundlessness of his own power and the depth of his own soul, a self long ago lost but now returned to reflect the image of me—the me I never chose to see, the me I never aspired to be.

It was a confrontation the likes of which I have never before known. A confrontation . . . but not a confrontation, for this presence brought an atmosphere of comfort, acceptance, and peace. It was OK to fall here. It was OK if you dropped the ball. You didn't have to be a winner. You didn't have to be a fighter. All you had to be was yourself.

I stood in awe of a living presence far beyond the limitations of my comprehension. There were no words to describe what I was witnessing. I was speechless.

I just watched, taking in the moment, as this being radiated it's presence. I was looking into the penetrating face of a long-forgotten truth—a truth I chose to abandon. I was face-to-face with myself— maybe for the first time in my life.

"For what do you wish?"

The words came from seemingly out of nowhere. I was being asked a question, though not a word was spoken. For they were not words you could hear; they were words that you felt. And I remember how he smiled when he asked, for he knew my answer before he asked the question.

I answered him with a thought: "I wish I was you."

"You *are* me," he answered. "You just haven't *realized* it yet. Know that when you awaken, I'm with you and I love you . . . always." He then slowly faded into the dark night sky. . . .

I was suddenly awakened to a presence I had never before encountered!

With this sudden awakening, I found myself lying face up in the gravel alongside the highway, right next to that old, abandoned car. The dark night sky was transformed into an explosion of light. For the first time in a long while, I felt really free. There was no fear of death, no fear of hurt, and no fear of loneliness. I was happy just to be here and alive with the hope that being me had some real possibilities.

I just laid there in a state of timeless nowness, watching everything. My inner storms were gone, quieted by new sense-abilities. I felt so much gratitude! In my darkest moment, a living presence revealed itself in its own unique way. It was a living presence that was actively functioning through what I called the disguise of life—from seemingly out of nowhere. It was a presence I had never before been aware of.

I was given a new vision of myself—a higher self. I came to realize later that there was no disguise of life. Life doesn't wear a disguise; people do. The only one wearing a disguise was me. For most of my life, I lived within the confines of an identity that really wasn't me.

It was an opportunity to see myself in a reality I never before perceived. I now call it my ultimate escape—an escape from a self-destructive mentality that poisoned my whole life.

I was at a loss for any logical reasons as to why all of this was revealed to me. That's when I realized that reason and logic had nothing to do with it. It was something bigger—something so big and so vast that forgiveness, understanding, mercy, and love were not the exception but the rule.

These principles were my new doorway to freedom—freedom from a self-destructive personality that shaped my world for as long as I could remember. My head was now swimming with these new possibilities.

I realized at that very moment that a whole new reality can blossom from the simple seed of a new perspective. I was now in touch with a *living presence* that had been there all along—a presence that emanated life. The gravel, the grass, the metal car, the asphalt road that stretched out to nowhere—we were all a part of the same living energy!

I was a witness to a *living state of ecstasy*—to something so awesome and spectacular that words could not come close to describing what I was experiencing. . . . What was this mysterious presence that revealed itself?

I now saw the fallacy of the old way of life I had chosen. I came to see that rebellion in itself, serves no purpose if it hides you from the truth of your own heart. For me, this understanding proved to be some sort of an answer. I thought about the sheer beauty of my encounter with my higher self and the powers at work behind the single star that revealed itself in my moment of darkness.

Could something as remotely obscure as a single star in the night sky have some overall meaning that no one outwardly recognizes?

Could it be that the darkness we're all so afraid to face is nothing more than a doorway to the light of new understanding? I really don't know. I guess it's really all in how you look.

You see, it's the work of the search

that led me to see

that the key to the truth

all along was with me!

And it wasn't in a book or a bible or a doctrine or a philosophy. It was a *living presence* responding to life—my life! I looked deep into my past and realized that presence was always there, saving me from countless situations. Changing and influencing my life at far deeper levels than I was consciously aware. It was there all along, responding from out of nowhere.

It was there when the police came to the fight in the park. And no one got hurt or arrested.

It was there when Dianna, my first love, appeared in the bowling alley. From out of nowhere, that subtle, unforeseen presence was always there— molding, shaping and influencing my world.

It was more than mere coincidence. It was ... miraculous!

———————

I used to believe I could escape from most anything when in fact I was *rescued—rescued from out of nowhere* by subtle, unforeseen forces far outside the boundaries of my comprehension or control. Without being aware, I was saved countless times by a presence whose gracefulness and mercy know no bounds—a nameless, faceless presence that existed far beyond the boundaries of words and thought.

My gratitude for this insight has forever changed my life.

The old man's words once again came to mind: Be aware. Be aware. Without realizing it, he gave me the key, the absolute answer, that rescued me from a self-destructive mentality and a self-destructive way of life.

It isn't just about survival. It's about being truly connected to life—a real, tangible, living connection to everything—a holy presence that we're all a part of but not conscious of. A graceful, mystical presence that for some unknown reason revealed itself in my darkest moment, from out of nowhere, when I had nothing left to hang on to.

Maybe that was life's intention all along—to open the door to the gift, the present; to let go and let be; to recognize the present that life truly is. Maybe it's the only rule I ever needed.

———

I was still lying on the gravel by the side of the road when a subtle movement caught my attention from out of the corner of my eye. It was a cockroach. I watched as he scampered around doing whatever it is that cockroaches do. He was totally unaware of me as I continued to observe his behavior. He seemed preoccupied, flittering from place to place.

I thought about my last cockroach encounter when he suddenly stopped and looked at me. We were somehow locked into this odd moment of mutual recognition when the strangest thought shot into my brain. It was a personal message from the roach directly to me: Welcome back, ya big asshole!

I laughed at the thought. How could I help but see myself from his perspective? He was right. I was an asshole. Piss-on-the-roach is not a game that roaches are fond of.

I never felt the need to apologize to a cockroach, but after a night like tonight, it seemed appropriate. An apology was in order. So I apologized. It was a strange ending to an even stranger night.

To this day, I'm not sure if the thought was the roach's or mine. But at the time, I couldn't help but acknowledge the profoundness of the moment. Wow! Humbled by a cockroach! I guess I had it comin'.

CHAPTER 30

The sun was starting to pierce the horizon. . . . I sat up and brushed myself off. It truly was the dawn of a new day. I started walking. I walked and walked until I came to an exit ramp that eventually led to a truck stop.

As I walked into the restaurant section, everyone in the place stared at me. I must have looked like something the cat dragged in.

"Good morning, ladies and gentleman," I shouted and headed straight for the men's room.

I looked in the mirror and realized why everyone was staring. My reflection was a shock to me as well. I thought about being thrown out of the ambulance the night before. No wonder I freaked out the ambulance attendant!

I stared at myself in the mirror and spoke to my reflection: "What would Elvis do with this mess?"

I took off my shirt and cleaned up at the sink. I brushed off my clothes, combed my hair, and straightened myself up. It was time to show the world a new me.

When I exited the men's room, a transformation had taken place. What I felt on the inside was starting to show on the outside.

I sat down at the counter and looked inside my wallet. There was just enough money for a cup of coffee. I put the money on the table and reached back to put my wallet away when I heard a familiar voice.

"Three eggs over easy, a beef patty medium, rye toast, coffee, and a glazed doughnut." It was Gert!

I jumped up and hugged her over the counter. "Gert, how are you?" I think I surprised her with my spirited greeting.

"How are you, stranger," she answered. "And what are you doing on this side of the river?"

"It's a long story," I explained. "And I have to tell you, it's only coffee today. I'm a little short."

"Don't worry, sweet pea. You look like you could use a break. You look like hell."

"I was closer than you know."

Gert fed me my usual breakfast, and I thanked her for the break. We talked about the old neighborhood and old times. It felt like those times were a thousand years ago. Both of our lives had taken us a long way from home. I didn't comment on it, but I was pretty sure Gert felt the same way. She didn't mention the shooting at the Swagger In or the robbery at her diner, so I brought it up.

"Gert, I'm sorry you lost your diner like that. I know you loved that place, and I'm sorry things went down the way they did."

"Everything happens for a reason, sweet pea. The old neighborhood was getting too dangerous, and I was too stubborn to leave. I'm lucky I lived through the robbery and nobody else got hurt.

"The man I shot turned out to be a really dangerous hombre. He was a member of one of the most vicious gangs in the country. The police warned me that my life was in danger. They said there were repercussions for taking his life. I felt like I had no other choice than to close it up and leave. I lost my business and my livelihood, but I walked away with my life. That's more than he got away with."

"I remember after the police arrived, they took your pistol as evidence. How are you going to protect yourself without a gun?"

Gert gave me a wink and said, "What makes you think that's the only one?"

I cracked up!

"Why are you laughing?" Gert said in her Gert the Guru tone. "A girl's got a right to defend herself."

"Good for you, Gert. I'm glad you found a way to get past it."

Gert's face grew serious. "You're never past it. There's not a day goes by that I don't think about it."

I could tell this conversation was starting to upset her, but I felt the need to continue. Both of us faced life altering tragedy. It was our common thread. I felt compelled to ask another question.

"So how do you resolve it?"

Gert the Guru spoke. "There's nothing to resolve. It resolved itself when he stuck that gun in my face and pistol-whipped me."

"Are you sorry he died?"

"No, I'm not sorry. He was wrong when he stuck that gun in my face. He was wrong when he took the cash out of my register. He was wrong when he robbed and threatened my customers. And he was wrong when he thought I wouldn't do anything about it.

"I made a decision in the moment, and I have to live with it for the rest of my life. I live with the memory of it every day, but I'm not sorry.

"When it comes right down to it, we both lost. I lost my livelihood, and he lost everything. Maybe we were both wrong. I don't really know about right or wrong anymore, but I'm grateful I'm still here to reflect on it.

"It was the worst day of my life, and it has changed me—that much is certain. I took a life that day. It's the worst feeling in the world. That's the price I pay every day. But in that split second, I chose to take a stand, and for that I'm not sorry. That's how I live with it, sweet pea."

Gert refilled my coffee. She hesitated before she spoke. "I read about you in the papers. The shooting was all over the news. So how do *you* live with it?"

"I have regrets," I said, "but I've since been shown a better way. I pray I can be open to it."

"Good for you sweet pea, I hope you find peace in your life."

"I found a whole lot more than that, but I don't know what to say about it."

"Then don't say anything about it." Gert said as she refilled my coffee. "Sometimes it's best to keep it to yourself."

"Maybe so."

Gert left me alone to finish my breakfast. I was hungry and the food tasted wonderful. What a great day! The restaurant was charged with the vigorous high energy of nine-to-fivers caught up in the hustle and bustle of the everyday work week. I sat there for awhile, enjoying the feeling of fullness, and the high energy atmosphere. I hated to leave, but it was time to go.

"Gert, seeing you again has made my day. I can't begin to tell you how much this conversation meant to me. Thank you so much for everything."

I slid my last two dollars across the counter, but she wouldn't take it. I thanked her again and told her I somehow misplaced my car.

Gert thought that was rather humorous. She called over to one of the truckers and asked if he would give me a ride across the river.

The trucker's name was Sal. Sal was a fifty-year-old South-sider who lived close to the neighborhood where I grew up. We hit it off right off the bat. Once he found out where I lived, he agreed to give me a ride. As it turned out, Sal was happy for the company. We didn't talk a lot, but it was a comfortable ride none the less.

I had never been in a tractor-trailer before. Riding down the highway, way up in the cab, gave me a whole new perspective of the road. It was a higher vision, the second higher vision I received in the last two days. How about that!

Sal offered to take me all the way to my studio, but I wouldn't let him. Truckers are on a time schedule, and I didn't want to throw him off of his. He had already gone out of his way to help me.

He dropped me off on the side of the highway, less than a mile from my place. I thanked him for the ride, and we shook hands. Before I got out of the cab, I told him I would gladly return the favor if he ever needed me for anything.

Sal reminded me of my dad. He was a hard worker and a straight shooter, someone you could trust on his word.

As I closed the door of his truck, I thanked him again for the ride and wished him good luck. I felt like I made a new friend.

CHAPTER 31

I walked the rest of the way home, climbed the iron staircase, and made my way into my studio. After a long, hot shower, I dried off and crashed on the bed. It was quite a night and quite a morning.

I thought about my unexpected encounter with Gert and my free ride home. That's all I really wanted! And it all came together when I least expected it, from seemingly out of nowhere.

I came to realize there are no coincidences—that everything in my life, both the good and the bad, led me to a moment of great awakening. And through it all, I somehow made a connection with a higher way of being.

I feel total gratitude for the *all* of it—even the bad times. God and the universe work in mysterious ways.

I thought about divine intervention and the nightmare of events that unfolded in my life. I thought about Adriana, my mother, and Rubin, and the scars I will forever carry from that unforgettable night. The memory will forever be with me, but it will no longer rule my life.

You see, I escaped from life and I escaped from death, but I couldn't escape from love. It was right there all along. Throughout my whole life, I was guided and embraced by the open arms of a benevolent all-knowing presence in spite of my self-destructive tendencies. I was just too blind to see. The words *thank you* don't come close to describing my gratitude.

So there it is. . . . I escaped from a self-destructive way of life into a whole new reality. A reality filled with hope, promise, and the possibility of a better way to be. It was truly a new beginning and the ultimate self-transformation.

And yes, the escape artist still lives within me. But I no longer crucify his existence, and he no longer tries to crucify mine. There's no need. For the acceptance of his ever-watchful presence is a miracle in itself. And somewhere in that acceptance lies my peace.

I guess you could say we're friends now. And I have to say, I respect him for getting me through the hard times. . . .

And the ghosts of my past? They're all there, too. But they don't bother me so bad. Besides, if you fuck with a fly on the ceiling, that's where you're at!

Flies on the ceiling . . .

I stood at my sink, looking out my kitchen window, watching as a moth slammed into an overhead alley light. The night was clear and the moon was full, but the moth took no notice. Head first and full force, he slammed himself time after time into the light.

That's what happens once you catch a glimpse of the light. Once you taste the magic, you're never the same again.

Dianna taught me that—many, many years ago. . . . And sometimes . . . in quiet moments . . . when mind is clear and thoughts no longer clutter like children demanding attention … I remember her warmth and her softness and her presence. And I know that a part of her is still with me.

The people you love always stay with you—always!

You see, it was Dianna who first saw within me something that I couldn't see in myself. Something . . . honorable. . . . And for that,

I'll always be grateful . . . . And as for the poetry . . . for that, I have no explanation.

I continued watching through the window while the moth continued to slam himself into the light.

"Just let it go," I said. "You'll get there soon enough!"

But the moth wouldn't listen. He continued in his relentless pursuit to enter into the light.

"Just float!" I tried to tell him, but he just wouldn't listen.

This moth and I are brothers—this much I know.

I continued to watch as the moth refused to give up. It was painful to watch. He just couldn't help it. It was the only way he knew how to be.

For how long would this madness continue? How much suffering will he endure before he realizes there's a better way?

I was witnessing a reenactment of my former life. . . . The moth continued to demonstrate the limitations of my former self.

I wanted to reach out and help. After all, that's what happened to me. So I did the best I could. I called out—from out of nowhere.

"That's not how it's done. There's an easier way, a higher possibility."

It was a last-ditch effort to save him from unnecessary pain. But he just wouldn't listen.

I contemplated the futility of his hard-nosed approach. There was something very familiar in his relentless behavior.

But deep down, I understood. . . . Just another taste. That's all he wants—to be *touched*. Maybe that's all we're here for.

You know, it's kind of funny. All my life, I thought I was "touched." And up until now, I never knew what it meant. Touched, I guess it's true, because here I am, half broken and still a little crazy. But I ain't dead yet!

Yes . . . I'm touched. . . . But it didn't come sudden—no lightning bolts from heaven, no startling revelations, no mind-expanding explosions! It was something more subtle, gradual, like a soft illumination that slowly seeps in through midnight clouds.

Now, I look at the moon and laugh. . . .

Just a soft light, floating through darkness. That's all we really are!

Touched, yes . . . it's true. I was touched. For it was here—in the dark, quiet, emptiness of this very room—that I, the escape artist, made peace with the moon.

EPILOGUE

The escape artist watched life

through the window of his studio,

content with his view, his hot coffee,

and his worn-out stereo.

Johnny Rivers still played in his head.

Stretch still made him laugh.

Rubin still made him cry.

And Adriana still broke his heart.

But still, he loved the silence.

For it was in those moments

that the love and beauty of life

still came to him.

And it was in those moments

that he knew he was free.

ABOUT THE AUTHOR

Ray's thirty-year career in emergency services (Fire and EMS) placed him on the front lines of countless crises situations. It is from this unique perspective that the reader gets to witness the main character's descent into a whirlwind of personal tragedy and its eventual resolution.

Through the lead character's eyes, the reader experiences the apocalyptic repercussions and aftermath of life-altering events, and the transformational outcome that follows.

Through the creation of his character, the author delivers a strong authentic narrative in an honest straight forward self-revealing way.

An unusual tale, with an unexpected outcome—a must read!

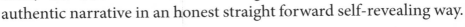

Made in the USA
Middletown, DE
06 December 2018